Books by Shirleen Davies

Historical Western Romance Series

MacLarens of Fire Mountain

Tougher than the Rest, Book One
Faster than the Rest, Book Two
Harder than the Rest, Book Three
Stronger than the Rest, Book Four
Deadlier than the Rest, Book Five
Wilder than the Rest, Book Six

Redemption Mountain

Redemption's Edge, Book One
Wildfire Creek, Book Two
Sunrise Ridge, Book Three
Dixie Moon, Book Four
Survivor Pass, Book Five
Promise Trail, Book Six
Deep River, Book Seven
Courage Canyon, Book Eight
Forsaken Falls, Book Nine
Solitude Gorge, Book Ten
Rogue Rapids, Book Eleven
Angel Peak, Book Twelve
Restless Wind, Book Thirteen
Storm Summit, Book Fourteen, Coming Next in the Series!

MacLarens of Boundary Mountain

Colin's Quest, Book One,
Brodie's Gamble, Book Two
Quinn's Honor, Book Three
Sam's Legacy, Book Four
Heather's Choice, Book Five
Nate's Destiny, Book Six
Blaine's Wager, Book Seven
Fletcher's Pride, Book Eight
Bay's Desire, Book Nine
Cam's Hope, Book Ten

Romantic Suspense

Eternal Brethren, Military Romantic Suspense

Steadfast, Book One
Shattered, Book Two
Haunted, Book Three
Untamed, Book Four
Devoted, Book Five
Faithful, Book Six, Coming Next in the Series!

Peregrine Bay, Romantic Suspense

Reclaiming Love, Book One
Our Kind of Love, Book Two
Edge of Love, Coming Next in the Series!

Contemporary Romance Series

MacLarens of Fire Mountain

Second Summer, Book One
Hard Landing, Book Two
One More Day, Book Three
All Your Nights, Book Four
Always Love You, Book Five
Hearts Don't Lie, Book Six
No Getting Over You, Book Seven
'Til the Sun Comes Up, Book Eight
Foolish Heart, Book Nine

Burnt River

Thorn's Journey
Del's Choice
Boone's Surrender

The best way to stay in touch is to subscribe to my newsletter. Go to www.shirleendavies.com and subscribe in the box at the top of the right column that asks for your email. You'll be notified of new books before they are released, have chances to win great prizes, and receive other subscriber-only specials.

Storm Summit

Redemption Mountain Historical Western Romance Series

SHIRLEEN DAVIES

Book Fourteen in the Redemption Mountain Historical Western Romance Series

Avalanche Ranch Press, LLC
PO Box 12618
Prescott, AZ 86304

Book design and conversions by Joseph Murray at 3rdplanetpublishing.com

Cover design by Kim Killion, The Killion Group

ISBN: 978-1-947680-16-6

I care about quality, so if you find something in error, please contact me via email at shirleen@shirleendavies.com

Description

A hardened lawman fighting the betrayal of the woman he loved.
The female agent who couldn't rid him from her heart.

Storm Summit, Book Fourteen, Redemption Mountain Historical Western Romance Series

Chandler Evans made the decision years ago to turn his back on a privileged life in New York to follow his older brother, Gabe, to the frontier. He didn't regret the decision to become a Texas Ranger, only the choices which went with it. His first mistake had been to accept a government agent as a partner. The second was to fall in love with a woman incapable of returning his emotions.

Agent Elizabeth Cartman became a widow much too young. Guilt plagued her, especially when feelings for a young Texas Ranger grew too strong to ignore. Retreat had been her lone option, running from her feelings easier than facing them. She never expected to see him again, but fate had other ideas.

Handing in his badge and riding north, Chan followed a precarious path to Splendor. Settling in as a U.S. Marshal, he obeyed a summons to Big Pine, finding himself face-to-face with the one woman he hoped had disappeared from his life forever.

Refusing the new assignment would achieve nothing, especially when a routine investigation turned to a game of life and death.

The hunters become the hunted, while the identity of the threat continues to elude them. As their mutual attraction grows, rekindling what they'd lost years before, they find themselves facing direct attacks to them and those they care about.

Can two fiercely independent people find a way to accept their love while fighting those intent on driving them apart by any means necessary?

Storm Summit, book fourteen in the Redemption Mountain historical western romance series, is a full-length novel with an HEA and no cliffhanger.

Visit my website for a list of characters for each series.
http://www.shirleendavies.com/character-list.html

Storm Summit

Prologue

Austin, Texas
September 1868

Chandler "Chan" Evans tightened his hold around the naked woman in his bed, content and at peace. The woman he'd made love to over the last few weeks, and more than once tonight, slept soundly beside him.

Chan had no idea when first meeting Federal Agent Elizabeth Cartman he'd fall in love with her. All he'd felt was frustration and anger at the government for sending in a female to help the Texas Rangers track down three bank robbers from New York. Specifically, to help him.

It had been his assignment until Cartman showed up. He'd already tracked the men to a small town several days' ride north of Austin, the Rangers' headquarters. All he'd requested was another man to assist him in the arrest. He had no use for an agent who wore a skirt and displayed twin six-shooters around her tiny waist.

They made quite a pair. Chan at over six feet tall, Beth at five-foot-six. He was muscled and broad-shouldered, dwarfing her petite, feminine frame. People gravitated toward Beth, while most took a step away when spotting him.

After figuring out there'd be no chance of handling the case alone, he'd accepted a partnership was inevitable. She'd been more obstinate. Difficult didn't begin to describe their tense relationship.

It had taken several days and more than one argument before they'd developed a bit of respect for each other. Respect had changed to a tentative friendship before they'd become lovers, working together to arrest and escort the robbers back to Austin.

Brushing fingers over her bare shoulder and down her arm, he didn't want to admit how much Beth had come to mean to him. He'd fallen in love, and from what he could tell, she returned his affection.

They hadn't discussed a future, but he felt certain there would be one. Chan had already prepared himself to counter any objections she might have, certain their emotional connection would endure.

Closing his eyes on the wondrous thought of spending the rest of his life with the woman in his arms, Chan let out a contented breath.

A few hours later, early morning sun streaming between the slight opening in the curtains, he reached across the bed, searching for Beth's warm body. Instead, he'd felt emptiness and cold sheets. Hours old cold sheets.

Hurrying to slip into his clothes, he left the bedroom of his small home, expecting to find her in the kitchen with a cup of coffee and one of her dime novels. Instead, he'd spotted a short note.

With a shaky hand, he picked it up, scanning it twice before the reality of her words sank in. Their brief time together was over. Beth was gone.

Chapter One

Splendor, Montana Territory
September 1870

U.S. Marshal Chan Evans rode alongside the herd of Texas longhorns, helping Dom Lucero and his men move them to a pasture farther north. His job as a marshal didn't take all his time, allowing him to live and work on the Lucero ranch when not performing duties as an officer of the law.

The hard, physical tasks suited him. After spending most of his life in what some would consider a mansion in New York, the simple chores of a cowhand gave him a sliver of peace.

He'd left the privileged life as the youngest of the four Evans' sons to follow his oldest brother. Gabe had been gone for years, forsaking the advantages of having a successful, businessman father to serve the Union during the war. Afterward, he'd ridden west with his close friend, Noah Brandt, searching for a new life.

They'd ended up in Splendor. Noah as a blacksmith and store owner, Gabe as the sheriff. By the time Chan left New York, spent time as a Texas Ranger, and tracked down his brother to the growing town in the western Montana Territory, both men had married.

Gabe had offered Chan a job as his deputy. The longer he'd thought about it, the less working for his brother appealed to him. When Dom left his position as a U.S. Marshal, he'd recommended Chan. It hadn't taken long to obtain approval from the powers in charge back east and be sworn in.

"We'll be driving them to the right a hundred yards ahead, Chan." Mal Jolly, Dom's foreman, rode beside him, his gaze focused on the herd.

He'd been one of the top hands at Redemption's Edge, the ranch owned by the Pelletier brothers. Bull Mason, one of their two foremen, recommended Mal to Dom after getting the approval of his bosses. The change had gone well, giving Mal the opportunity he'd been wanting while Dom ended up with an experienced man.

"How are you doing?" Mal asked.

Lifting one shoulder in a shrug, Chan grinned. "Getting used to them."

"Those six-foot horns can be intimidating."

From tip to tip, some of the horns could grow to almost seven feet. Dom had purchased a shorthorn bull and cows from the Pelletiers, intending to crossbreed. It could be a couple years to learn if the experiment would be successful. And if the herd brought from Texas could survive the freezing winters of Montana.

"Any news from the territorial capital?" Mal asked.

"Nothing yet. Judge Collins in Big Pine is planning a trial in a couple weeks. He'll send a telegram to let me know when I'm needed." Chan grinned again, showing straight, white teeth. "Until then, I'm *all* yours."

Mal grunted with a sharp shake of his head, kicking his horse to ride closer to the front of the herd. Chan went back to his own thoughts. Moving the cattle didn't take his complete concentration. Not with a herd of this size or his position at the right flank.

His job was to drive the herd forward while picking up and turning back any strays. The perfect spot for a man who wanted to think. It seemed recalling the past and forcing himself to consider his future took most of his mental capacity.

He'd always been a restless sort. His job as a Texas Ranger had suited him fine, as did his one as a marshal. Living in a bunkhouse with a group of men ranging from their teens to their sixties gave him ample amount of entertainment and insight.

They'd played cards, strummed their guitars, and told stories, which sounded unbelievable at times. The solemn expressions on the cowboys' faces after many of them told Chan there could be a good deal of truth to the tales.

Reaching the destination where the cattle would graze for the immediate future, he slid to the ground, reaching into his saddlebags. The same as the rest of the men, hardtack and jerky had become his main sustenance when away from the ranch house.

Josephine Dubois had married Dom a few months earlier, dividing her time between preparing meals for the ranch hands and the store she owned with her closest friend, Olivia Barnett. Their shop, Splendor Emporium, had been an instant success. The women offered items not sold at other places in town, at prices the locals could afford.

She'd rise each morning well before sunup and make meals for the men. Three days a week Josie rode to Splendor to work in the store. Olivia handled the work four days, with the two women overlapping on Fridays. Soon, Olivia would marry Doctor Clay McCord and they might need to make changes. For now, the schedule suited them both.

"When you heading out, Marshal?" An older, grizzled cowboy sat down next to him, breaking off a piece of hardtack.

"Not for a week or two, Curly." Chan held back a chuckle. He'd never asked how a man with a bald head could earn the name Curly.

"Another trial?"

Chan nodded, tearing off a small piece of jerky and chewing. "Unless I'm ordered back sooner. Sheriff Sterling is holding a man suspected of killing the sheriff in Moosejaw. He expects there to be a good number of people crowded inside the courtroom to watch the trial."

"Parker's a good man. And a cautious one."

Leaning back, Chan looked at him. "I didn't know you knew the Big Pine sheriff, Curly."

"I know a lot of people. Parker and I go way back. Could say we were babes together, but that wouldn't be quite true." Shoving his hat off his forehead, Curly drank from a canteen before capping it.

"What *is* true?"

Curly threw back his head and cackled. "I can see how you and Gabe are brothers. 'Cept you smile a lot more often."

Chan knew he and his oldest brother bore a strong resemblance. They also were the most restless of the four brothers. Both had left their secure surroundings to seek a different life far away from the bustling city of New York.

The difference was Gabe had always been more serious. Chan had been the jokester, the son who could get away with more than the others. An easy smile and brash manner got him through life quite well. Until he'd met Elizabeth Cartman.

After she'd disappeared, his smile didn't come so easy, although his brash attitude stayed intact. Brash and a little more jaded.

"I've been told that by a lot of people, Curly."

"Bet you have." He took another swallow of water, swiping an arm across his mouth.

Chan stretched out on the grassy ground, adjusting his hat to cover his eyes. "You have brothers?"

"Just a gaggle of sisters. All older. Might as well have had five mothers."

Chuckling, Chan thought of his other two brothers, Weldon and Lawrence. To his friends, Weldon was somber and straitlaced. They turned a blind eye to the mistress he'd taken not long after his marriage into another socially prominent family. Chan had never liked him and hoped to never see him again.

Lawrence held a position as an aide to a prominent New York State senator. Never married. Never intended to. Chan had always thought his brother preferred the company of men to women, but he'd never cared enough to bring up the subject.

They were welcome to the lives they'd chosen. All Chan asked was to have the same freedom. For now, he'd found it in Splendor.

"You gonna be riding into town this evening?" Curly asked.

"Plan to. Why? Do you have a letter to mail?"

"Matter of fact, I do. It's in the bunkhouse, under my mattress. Mal wants me to stay with the herd tonight."

"That's fine," Chan said. "I'll get it posted for you."

"Thanks, Marshal. Money's in the bunkhouse, too."

Chan waved a hand in the air. "I'll get it when I return to the ranch, Curly."

He heard Curly stand, then the sound of boots crunching on the ground when the older man walked away. Chan liked Curly, a taciturn cowboy whose word was his bond.

Sitting up, he shoved his hat back, settling it on his head as he stood. By the look of the sun, it was time he rode back to the ranch, cleaned up, and continued to town.

Gabe's wife, Lena, had invited him to supper. Chan and Gabe's father, Walter, and his friend, Baron

Klaussner, would also be there. He hoped Lena had invited his half-sister, Nora, and her husband, Wyatt Jackson. Wyatt worked for the Pelletiers at Redemption's Edge, breaking and training horses for their Army contracts.

Chan rode to the bunkhouse, changed into clean clothes, grabbed Curly's letter, and took the trail to Splendor. The late afternoon was clear and crisp, the dark blue sky dotted with a few white clouds. The ride relaxed him, had Chan thinking about how long he'd stay.

He had no great urge to move on. It hit him how strange it felt to consider making a life in the growing frontier town. The thought didn't panic him as he'd expected.

Chan had done well as a Texas Ranger because of the diverse nature of the job. He rarely stayed in one place more than a few days, always searching and hunting. Some fugitives gave up, others chose to fight. Chan survived each one, wounding or killing the men who resisted.

The urge to continue his search for Gabe had him turning in his badge. There were days Chan wondered if Beth had stayed, would they have built a life in Austin, Washington, D.C., New York, or someplace new. He didn't know why his mind drifted to what could never be, twisting his gut, souring his mood. Agent Cartman had made her choice.

Since her early morning departure two years earlier, he'd never spoken of Beth, or confessed to anyone how her leaving still tortured him. Chan had been with other women, none leaving an impression—good or bad. They'd just been women to share time with, nothing more.

Seeing the edges of the town up ahead, he watched in fascination as a wagon loaded with a large, enclosed crate entered the main street. Gabe told him about a similar package which had been delivered to a shop in Chinatown almost a year earlier. It had taken ten men to unload and carry it into one of the stores. Gabe had assumed it was a stove or another piece of equipment needed to make a living.

Chan waved at deputies Caleb Covington and Mack Mackey as he rode past the jail. The town was growing, and he knew Gabe was looking for more help. As far as Chan could tell, his deputies were worth at least three of most other men.

Turning onto a side street, he slowed his buckskin gelding, Caesar, keeping a good distance between himself and the wagon.

Ten men lowered the crate from the wagon, struggling with the weight. When satisfied they wouldn't drop it, the men moved it into a shop as the wagon moved on.

Curious, Chan reined Caesar past the store, but the windows were too dirty to see what the crate held. Deciding he didn't have time to enquire, and knowing

Gabe wouldn't appreciate him riling the locals, he swung his gelding around to retrace his route.

As much as he enjoyed his time on Dom's ranch, Chan was ready for an assignment sooner rather than later. The man in Sheriff Sterling's jail would go to trial in about two weeks. Most trials in the territorial capital occurred within days of a person's arrest.

He wondered at the delay, reminding himself the crime was murdering a well-liked and respected sheriff in Moosejaw. Both sides would need time to prepare their cases. Chan found himself hoping another crime would be committed, requiring his presence sooner than two weeks.

Approaching the jail, he slowed at the sight of two women he'd never seen talking with Caleb and Mack. Both were dressed in clothing more appropriate in New York than Splendor, their hats extravagant, gloves still white instead of the more common dirty gray from the dust permeating the air.

One of the women raised her head, flashing Chan a welcoming smile, the other ignoring him. They had to have arrived within the last few days. Curiosity sparked again.

If anyone would know about newcomers to Splendor, it would be Lena and Gabe. Touching the brim of his hat with a finger, he returned the woman's smile, grinning when she blushed. How long had it been since he'd seen a woman blush? A long, long time.

Following the wagon had presented two mysteries. What were the shop owners in Chinatown unloading, and who were the two attractive women?

Chan felt a measure of satisfaction. The unease of not having a current assignment gave way to a feeling of anticipation. He now had two mysteries to solve. Both may be insignificant, taking little time, but they gave him enough of a rush to keep him going until he was called to Big Pine.

Chapter Two

Secret Service Agent Elizabeth Cartman held the Colt .32 pocket revolver in front of her. Ten yards away, a large, red "X" painted on a piece of wood identified her target. Aiming, she pulled the trigger, tearing off splinters but not hitting the mark.

"Raise the gun, Beth." Thaddeus Taylor stood a few feet behind her and to her left. He owned the property where the makeshift firing range had been erected, allowing the agents under his command a place to practice. Thad wasn't only her senior agent, but a good friend.

Doing as he suggested, Beth aimed again, hitting the bottom edge of the target. Not where she wanted. Dissatisfied, she leveled the revolver once more, raised the gun a little higher, and squeezed the trigger.

"Excellent," Thad said. "You have two shots left."

She'd selected the five shot derringer revolver because of its size and ability to load more than two or three rounds. The twin revolvers she used to carry were too big, too heavy. The new gun could be hidden in a pocket of a dress or coat, or slid into her reticule. Granted, the purse had been made of heavy tapestry using the dimensions of the weapon. Beth had liked it so much she'd ordered two more.

"Do you plan to stand there the rest of the morning, or are you going to fire off the last two bullets?"

She shot a disgruntled look at Thad, knowing he was trying to rile her. He thrived on teasing her, doing what he could to lighten her mood. Thad had been doing it since her husband died in the line of duty four years before. Abner had been his best friend, as well as hers.

They'd been married a short year before an assignment went wrong. She'd watched it happen, unable to stop the bullet from piercing Abner's chest. The fact Beth killed the shooter did nothing to comfort her. She'd lost the love her life in a dark, damp alley in the back streets of New York.

Raising her arm, she cocked the hammer, aimed, and pulled the trigger, then again, emptying her gun. Both bullets hit the target within inches of center. They were good, clean shots. Beth lowered the gun, feeling a wave of satisfaction.

"You owe me lunch, Thad."

"I'll gladly buy."

"And I get to choose the restaurant."

An amused grin tipped the corners of his mouth. "Agreed."

Motioning her to follow, they walked through the spacious grounds of his New York home, through the house to the parlor. "I'll call for the buggy while you decide where to go."

"Delmonico's."

Thad looked at her a moment before he threw back his head and laughed. "I should've guessed. I'll call for a carriage."

Beth watched him disappear into the bowels of the large home, no doubt searching for his butler. Taking a seat on one of two settees, she let herself relax.

Thaddeus Taylor descended from a prominent New York family who'd made their fortune in shipbuilding, commerce, and finance. His father and uncles had been considered social elites, talented men with the drive to fulfill their dreams.

Thad had been poised to follow them. Then the war happened. His father had helped arrange a position for him within Lincoln's White House. He'd worked a few years for Allan Pinkerton, rising to senior investigator, meeting Abner during this time. And eventually, Beth.

The three had been almost inseparable, personally and professionally. She and Abner had married, continued their partnership when President Andrew Johnson signed the document establishing the U.S. Secret Service. She'd been one of two women who'd received an invitation. Beth had always suspected it was due to Abner threatening to resign if they didn't accept her.

"The carriage is ready." Thad stood before her, an indulgent expression on his face. She hadn't heard him approach, a mistake a novice would make.

The ride to Delmonico's didn't take long. Beth loved the building on South William Street, had eaten there half a dozen times. The food was exceptional, the service excellent, and the ambiance beyond anywhere else she'd ever been.

As she exited the carriage, her mind wandered to an evening two years before. Her lover had taken her to the fanciest restaurant in Austin, Texas. It had been one of the most wonderful evenings of her life. They'd worn their best clothes, eaten until barely able to breathe, then returned to his small home on the edge of town to make love.

She *had* loved him. It was the reason Beth had slid from the bed in the early morning hours, dressed, written a cryptic message, and left him behind. She'd fallen in love and hadn't been able to deal with the guilt of replacing Abner with another man, no matter how perfect.

Texas Ranger Chan Evans had been more than perfect. If he hadn't, she might have stayed longer.

Beth didn't know walking into Delmonico's would trigger this memory. All she felt was the sharp jolt to her heart.

"I received a message from headquarters," Thad said after they'd finished and were on their way back to his home, enjoying one of the few weekends without an assignment.

As was their custom, she'd often use one of his guest rooms when they weren't following a job. Most of the time, Thad would escort one of his lady friends to supper, then the theater or symphony. When he had the urge, he'd rent a room at one of the grand hotels for a discreet night alone.

Tonight, he didn't go back out. "Let's talk in the study."

The opulent room was more of a large, well-kept library with overstuffed chairs, decanters of brandy, and expensive glassware. He poured her a brandy and a whiskey for himself, handing her a glass.

She sat down, took a swallow of her drink, and waited. By experience, Beth knew Thad would tell her about the message in his own time. Tonight, he seemed conflicted. Either by the message or his reaction to whatever it said.

Minutes passed. She took another sip of brandy, laid her head against the back of the chair, and closed her eyes. Beth had learned to never let orders from headquarters bother her.

Thad was different. He asked questions of his supervisor before going directly to the president. Right now, the office was held by Ulysses S. Grant. Ex-Union general and war hero, at least to those who served the North. Because of Thad's background and status, Grant always made time for him, answered questions, and came to a decision.

Beth wondered what part of the message bothered him now, and if he'd fight them by going directly to the president. At some point, the tactic would end his career. Just not while Grant held the office.

Hearing Thad clear his throat, she opened her eyes and sat up.

"The chief has sent additional orders." He referred to Colonel H.C. Whitley, the head of the Secret Service and Thad's direct boss. "There's another new source of counterfeit money circulating."

"From where?"

"No one knows. We have no leads, no idea where the bills originated, or who's behind it. It was as if a tornado passed over the western U.S. and dropped bank notes."

"Where do they suggest we go?" Beth asked.

"A large number of the fake notes ended up in Texas. Specifically, Austin."

Her stomach clenched, chest squeezing at the mention of the last place she'd seen Chan. The last place she ever wanted to see again. At least that was what she'd been telling herself for two years.

"President Grant *suggested* Whitley send an agent to Austin, ask questions, the same as we've been doing on this case for almost a year," Thad said.

"It takes time to build a case of counterfeiting. Finding the source sometimes seems impossible."

"True."

"Are the bills confirmed forgeries?"

"The authorities in Austin sent some of them to the Treasury Department. They confirmed the bills are fake. More interesting, they're from more than one national bank."

This got her attention. Forgers rarely changed the original engravings as it took too much time and cost more. They'd select one of the federally chartered national banks, make the plates, and start printing.

"More than one?" Beth asked.

"Four different banks. Two different denominations. Ten dollar and one dollar notes."

Sitting forward, she finished the brandy and set down the empty glass. "Which ones?"

"Ten dollar bills from First National Bank of Atchison, Kansas, and San Antonio National Bank. One dollar bills from First National Bank of Pekin, Illinois, and Louisiana National Bank of New Orleans. These we can confirm. Who knows what other notes are being forged. Nothing has changed. It's our job to discover anything more and shutdown the forgers. Treasury has already sent notices to the four banks. We have a meeting with headquarters tomorrow morning, so have your questions ready."

Standing, she stretched her arms over her head, yawning. "It's going to be pretty long."

"If you haven't noticed, we're given some of the most difficult assignments. Important, but scarce information. Abner was an expert at mining concealed information helpful on a case."

The mention of her late husband, and Thad's close friend, had the conversation stalling. The same had happened several times since his death. Each time, there'd been a few awkward moments before they'd shaken off the shadow of his presence. It became easier over the years.

"Assuming this is all we get." She nodded to the paper in Thad's hand. "How would Abner approach it?"

The tension broken, he read the memorandum again, rubbing fingers across his brow. "He'd already be on his way to Austin to work the clues, questioning everyone who knew anything about the counterfeit bills. Slow, tedious, and necessary."

"Eventually, he'd track down the people behind it, arrest them, and move on to the next assignment," Beth said.

"The best agent we've ever had."

Lifting her empty glass, she tilted it toward him. "Yes, he was. So, where does that leave us?"

"My recommendation is we have our meeting tomorrow and decide how to go forward."

Walking toward the door, Beth stopped, glancing over her shoulder. "I agree."

Taking the stairs to her bedroom, she stepped inside, closing the door to stare at the bed. She and Abner had stayed in this room often during their year of marriage. They'd made love many times. Against the wall, on the thick, Aubusson rug, in the bed.

Undressing, she thought of the last time before his life ended. It had been slow, sweet, intoxicating. Almost as if Abner had expected it to be their last coupling.

After his funeral, she'd gone to bed each night for almost two years crying in remembrance. Then Beth had been sent on assignment to assist a Texas Ranger to apprehend three men who'd stolen money from one of the relatively new national banks.

Crawling under the covers, she stared at the ceiling, clutching the sheet to her chest, thinking about Chan Evans. They butted heads, argued, granted each other grudging respect. For the first time since Abner's death, she'd felt alive.

When they'd become lovers, it seemed a natural progression of the bond formed while sharing dangerous work. Initially, it was odd being with a man other than Abner. But he was dead, had been grieved for over two years.

Chan had known all about her husband's death. For a younger man who'd never been married, he understood the emotions of her trying to move on with her life. They'd talked about everything except the future, which was fine with her.

Then the guilt and fear of loving again had eclipsed her desire to be with Chan. She'd fled, leaving a short note. He'd deserved so much more.

Continuing to stare at the ceiling, she told herself it had been the right decision at the time. Two years later, it felt as if it had been the worst choice of her life.

Beth had convinced herself she couldn't possibly fall in love so soon after Abner. When she did, it wouldn't be with a Texas Ranger living halfway across the country. A man four years her junior.

Sighing, she turned onto her side, drawing the covers around her. Some decisions couldn't be undone. Her departure from Chan was one of them.

Chapter Three

Splendor

Chan focused on the red wine in the glass he held, watching the liquid change colors depending on how he tipped it to the light.

He'd begun to doubt his decision to invite the woman he'd spotted talking with Caleb and Mack to supper. Worse, he'd talked Zeke Boudreaux, another of his brother's deputies, into accompanying the second woman. Chan had been avoiding the piercing looks from Zeke since not long after they'd been seated at a table in the Eagle's Nest.

Beautiful with melodic voices, their appearance created fantasies for most men who encountered them. According to Lena and Nora, the women dressed in the latest fashions, wore the perfect amount of makeup, and offered practiced smiles, which he and Zeke had been treated to from the time they'd met them in the hotel lobby.

Chan's attraction to the taller of the two ended minutes after they'd been seated. Pretty as a picture. Dumb as a rock. Vapid in a way he hadn't experienced since attending social functions back in New York. Perfect hostess while being an unenticing partner. Another reason he'd left the populous city where everyone of consequence knew the Evans family.

The women droned on about the parties the two had attended back east, unending dust while traveling west, and their ultimate destination of San Francisco. They planned to stay in town several more days. Chan found himself wishing they'd be on the stage tomorrow.

At least he'd be gone. Sheriff Parker Sterling had sent him a reprieve in the form of a telegram the previous day. Chan was needed in Big Pine in four days.

His saddlebags were already packed, Caesar sleeping in a stall at Noah Brandt's livery. He'd arrive a day early, pay for a room at the Imperial Hotel, eat, play cards at one of several saloons, then select one of the fine women to take upstairs.

Sipping the wine, he set down his glass, his attention latching onto Zeke's. He owed his friend for talking him into what turned out to be a wasted evening. Especially given it was the deputy's night off. Since Zeke's brother, Hex, had returned to town with a daughter no one knew he had, the deputies had changed their schedules.

Hex worked days while Lucy was in school or with Isabella Travis. Zeke worked nights, giving his brother and his niece much needed time together. She'd turned five over the summer, allowing the precocious blonde, blue-eyed terror to occupy a desk in Sarah Murton's classroom.

It had only been two weeks and Hex had been asked to speak with Miss Murton several times. Most locals believed it didn't mean Lucy had been in trouble. A nice woman with hope for the future, the teacher was known to focus her attention on eligible bachelors, doing what she could to get close to them.

The reason didn't matter. What did was Chan taking away Zeke's one night to do what he pleased. Dessert couldn't come soon enough.

Big Pine

"The prisoner is tight-lipped. Eats, sleeps, and not much else. He doesn't want a lawyer, which is odd considering he shot a lawman." Sheriff Sterling didn't move from his spot behind the massive oak desk at the jail, hitching his thumb to point to the cells in back. "There are witnesses. Guess he figures his time on this earth is over."

Chan sat across from him, legs stretched out in front of him, ankles crossed. "Or he's thinking about escape."

Sterling nodded blandly. "I thought of that. No one has come to visit, and the witnesses don't remember him being with anyone at the saloon in Moosejaw."

"Is that where he shot the sheriff?"

"He and another man were arguing over a card game. They fought, carrying it out to the street. The sheriff tried to break it up. The man in the cell drew a gun and fired. Caught the sheriff in the heart. He was dead before hitting the ground."

"How far away was the shooter from the sheriff?"

Sterling reached into a drawer, reading from a piece of paper. "Witnesses said the prisoner was about twenty feet away."

"Why did it take so long to come to trial? It's been almost a month, right?"

"The judge and his wife were back east," Sterling said. "They didn't return until a few days ago."

"Are you expecting any trouble during the trial?"

"No reason to. The prisoner has had no visitors, made no threats."

"Has he said he's innocent?" Chan asked, surprised a man would meekly go through a trial without any support, including a lawyer.

"Nope. All he asks for are books to read and a bath once a week. Other than those, he rarely talks. Even says *please* and *thank you*." Sterling scratched his stubbled jaw. "Most polite prisoner I've ever met."

Chan felt a surge of unease sweep over him. It always happened when something made no sense.

A murder with several witnesses. A prisoner who didn't seem to care he faced hanging. A man who'd killed the sheriff with one clean shot to the heart. Not easy from twenty feet away.

Chan had seen it before. A practiced gunslinger could bring down an opponent at that distance. It took skill and a steady hand. Or luck.

"Tell me what's bothering you, Evans."

Without shifting his relaxed posture, Chan shrugged. "I don't know. Sometimes things don't add up to me. There's probably nothing wrong. I'm a cautious man, Sheriff."

"Can't blame you. Truth is, you'll be protecting the judge and jurors."

"We both know you'll be right there with me." Pulling his feet under him, Chan stood. "I've got a reservation at the Imperial Hotel for supper in an hour. Do you want to join me?"

"You buying?"

Chan shot a smug expression at Sterling before giving a curt nod and leaving the jail.

He'd planned a quiet supper, cards, and an evening in a room upstairs in a saloon. Instead, he and Sterling had discussed topics ranging from statehood for Montana, to their opinions on President Grant, to the constitutional amendment giving former slaves the right to vote, to Georgia's readmittance to the union.

They'd agreed on most, disagreed on others. It reminded him of the times his father and brothers had tackled complicated topics after supper. Chan had been young, but Walter Evans expected him to participate. The talks ended not long after Gabe joined the Union cause and left home.

When finished, he'd no longer been in the mood for cards or time with an unknown woman. So he lay in bed, curtains open, watching the moon through the window, his mind on Beth. More often than not, his nights ended the same way.

Chan didn't want anyone else. Even if he'd shared time with a handful of women since she disappeared, his thoughts always went back to her. Trim with an athletic body, smart with a quick wit and easy laugh, a dedicated federal agent with a feisty temper.

Blowing out a curse, he turned onto his side, punching the pillow. Damn woman still controlled his mind after two years, and Chan was tired of it.

A blast of what sounded like dynamite rocked his hotel room. Throwing off the covers, he hurried to the window. Down the street, smoke billowed from the jail's front door. A man backed outside, gun held in front of him, then dropped to the ground from the impact of a bullet.

Jamming his legs into his pants, not bothering with a shirt or boots, he secured his gunbelt while running down the stairs. Other than a few brave souls, few people stood outside. The ones who did stared at the jail.

Rushing across the street, Chan made his way down the boardwalk, bending low, his gun ready. Hearing a wave of whoops, he ran between two buildings, stopping at the next street. A group of riders headed south, shooting over their shoulders. He didn't know at who, since no one appeared to be following them.

Reaching the back of the jail, he stared at the gaping hole. Inside, the cell where the prisoner had been held was empty.

Chan stepped over the crumbling debris, checking each cell as he made his way to the front. Empty.

Stepping onto the boardwalk, he stared at the unmoving man being treated by a doctor. Beside them knelt Parker Sterling. Glancing up to see Chan, he stood and walked toward him, features grim.

"Doc thinks he'll recover. May have to shoot with his other hand and will have a helluva scar. He's my youngest deputy. I went to his wedding not more than a month ago." Sterling looked past Chan, into the wreckage. "The sonofabitch destroyed my jail."

"It can be rebuilt. What we need to figure out is who broke him out and where they went."

Stepping inside, he walked to the back, cursing again while surveying the damage. "The mayor isn't going to like this."

"You have an injured deputy and a destroyed jail. Do you care what the mayor thinks?" Chan slid the six-shooter into its holster.

"Never have cared for the man or what he thinks. He's a friend of the judge. I *do* care about that."

Chan came up beside him. Two cells destroyed, three more needing a serious amount of repair. The clean-up would take at least three days with several men.

"Might be easier to rebuild down the street."

Sterling nodded, not answering as he continued to survey the wreckage. He lifted what was left of the mangled iron bedframe.

"Our blacksmith finished this a few months ago. He made all five. It took me months to get the city council to approve the expenditure, but the prisoners were tearing the wood ones apart. Sure do hate to see this."

"The other four are in decent condition, Sheriff."

"I've been trying to get the council to approve the building of a new jail for over two years. After this, they'll have no choice."

"What the hell happened, Sterling?"

Both turned at the deep, raspy voice to see the judge, flanked by the mayor and two other men.

"Prisoner escaped, Judge."

"I can see that." Stepping over the rubble, he moved next to them. "Guess the man had friends after all."

"Seems so," Sterling said.

"I counted at least six riding away, Judge."

The older man's attention turned toward Chan. "Good to see you, Marshal Evans. You saw them?"

Chan looked out the gaping hole in the back wall. "They were already a quarter mile away when I got here. There was nothing I could do."

Judge Collins stared down at Chan's bare feet. "Be pretty hard to follow without boots."

"Or a horse, sir."

Chuckling, Collins motioned for the mayor and others to stay back. "You going to convene a posse and go after them, Sheriff?"

"Yes, sir."

Nodding, his gaze moved over the destruction once more. "Take Evans with you. I'll let the mayor know to expect a request for a new jail when you return. A request I can guarantee he'll approve."

Chapter Four

Splendor

Chan spun the cylinder of his gun, confirming it held six bullets, then set it on Gabe's desk. Still covered in trail dust, hungry, and thirsty, he'd ridden into town a few minutes earlier, heading straight to the jail.

"Five men blew a hole in the back of Sterling's jail, shot one of his deputies, and freed the prisoner before riding south. The posse followed for three days before we lost the trail."

"You were with them?" Gabe leaned back in his chair.

"Judge Collins asked me to go with them. Not sure why, as Sterling has some good deputies. It didn't matter if I was with them or not. They're probably in Colorado or Utah by now."

Gabe drew a stack of wanted posters from a drawer. Dividing them, he slid half toward Chan. "What's the man's name?"

"Simon Priest."

Gabe's hand stilled over his stack of posters. "Simon Priest? Are you certain?"

"Yes. Why?"

"Probably nothing. I heard about an officer in the Confederate Army during the war named Damien Priest. He was a colonel. The rumor was no one was more

33

dedicated to the Southern cause. Fought with a passion many men didn't have. He had a brother named Simon."

"How'd you hear about him?"

"The senior Priests were strong supporters of the North. I served with one of their neighbors." Gabe began to thumb through the posters. Halfway through the pile, he stopped, holding up one of them. "Simon Priest." Studying the illustration, his brows furrowed.

"Does he look like Damien?"

"Hard to tell. The colonel had a mustache and full beard. Simon has a mustache, but no beard." He handed the poster to Chan.

"I only saw him for less than a minute, but I'm certain this was the prisoner in Sterling's jail." Handing it back, he stared at his gun still on Gabe's desk. "Strange man. Sterling said he was the most polite prisoner he'd ever met. Read books. Had no visitors. It doesn't make sense."

"What?"

"Five men freed him, yet there's no mention on the poster about him being part of a gang. No one tried to free him from the Moosejaw jail before his transfer to Big Pine. Seems odd to me, Gabe."

Staring down at the illustration of Priest, Gabe said nothing for several long moments before slipping it back into the drawer. "I'll let my deputies know about Priest, but I doubt he'll come back this way. If he's smart, he'll have put a good distance between him and the Montana Territory."

Chan stood, holstering his gun. "I'll be heading back to the Lucero ranch."

"Lena's planning to invite you for supper again soon." Amusement crossed Gabe's face.

"Thought I already had a standing invitation to join you anytime."

"You do. This will be different."

A dark brow lifted. "How so?"

"Seems my wife thinks you need help finding an eligible woman."

Jaw dropping, Chan's incredulous expression was comical before his features sobered. "I don't need or want help finding a woman."

"Fair warning then. You may want to be prepared with an excuse the next time Lena asks you to join us."

One side of Chan's mouth tilted into a grin. "Message received, big brother. Thanks."

Stepping into the warm afternoon, he let out an amused breath. He loved his sister-in-law, but Lena's desire to take on the role of matchmaker could be frustrating.

Chan walked into the dark interior of the Dixie, taking a place at the bar. "A whiskey, Paul."

The longtime bartender slid a full glass in front of him. "Back from Big Pine?"

"For now." Taking a sip, he rested both arms on the bar.

"Bet you're ready to get back to the ranch and do some *real* work." Paul chuckled before leaving to serve another customer.

"Haven't seen you in a while, Chan." Nick Barnett, one of the saloon owners, came up next to him.

"Judge Collins called me to Big Pine."

"Another trial?"

Chan nodded, taking another sip. "The prisoner shot the sheriff in Moosejaw. Plenty of witnesses. He never set foot in the courtroom."

"Why's that?"

"A group of men busted him out of jail. Sterling's posse tried to follow, but we had to give up after three days."

"Do you think they're on their way here?" Nick's gaze flicked to the swinging front doors.

Chan gave a sharp shake of his head. "No. Their tracks showed them riding toward Wyoming. My guess is they continued south."

Nick lifted a shot of whiskey Paul had set before him. "Outlaws don't always do what you expect."

"How well I know."

Gyp Slade set his cards on the table, laughed, then scooped up his winnings. "Told you boys I'm feeling lucky."

"Feeling lucky and being lucky are two different things, Gyp." Hugh Fisher tossed back a whiskey, pouring another. Raising his voice to be heard over the tinny piano music a few feet away, he leaned toward Gyp. "This night isn't going to last long if you keep this up."

"That's my plan." He nodded to a curvy redhead moving toward them. "I've got places to be, Hugh. Do you boys have time to talk?"

Harvey Fisher smiled, winking at the lady waiting for Gyp. Standing, he followed his brother and Gyp to the empty end of the bar, taking his glass and bottle with him. Topping off each of their glasses, he set the bottle down.

"I get the impression you've got plans besides the lovely lady waiting for you," Hugh said, sipping his whiskey.

"I'm heading out tomorrow morning."

Hugh jerked. "Leaving? We just got here."

"Do you recall the U.S. Marshal who visited the jail?"

"Sure. We watched him from across the street. Someone called him Evans," Harvey said.

"Did he seem familiar to you?" Gyp asked, glancing at the woman he'd be taking upstairs when their conversation ended.

The brothers shot a look at each other, shaking their heads.

"Do you recall the man who rode into Cheyenne a year ago and disrupted our little party?"

Hugh's brows scrunched together. "Party?"

"Do you mean when we planned to hang that kid?" Harvey asked, not waiting for an answer. "Why would you want to track him down? He broke up what would've meant a good deal of money to us, then rode off."

"Because I aim to get our money back. From him."

Harvey gave an abrupt shake of his head. "It's not worth you riding up there, Gyp. Someone may recognize you as one of the men who got Priest out of jail."

"No one can identify us as the men who blasted a hole in the jail."

"Are you sure?" Hugh asked. "We had a good time at the saloon the night before." He waggled his brows. "A *real* good time, Gyp."

Drumming fingers on the bar in frustration, he poured more whiskey into his glass. "Then we rode out to our camp. We didn't return until the following night when we broke Priest out. Do either of you recall seeing anyone watching?"

"We got out of there real clean, Gyp," Harvey said.

"Then going back to find the marshal shouldn't be a problem."

The three fell silent for a few minutes, Hugh and Harvey sharing confused glances, Gyp content to drink before spending some time with the redhead.

"Anyone ever call you plumb crazy?" Hugh asked.

Gyp grinned. "You."

Hugh shifted to face him. "Priest has several jobs coming up. Any one of them will pay a lot more than anything you can get from that marshal fella. My vote is to wait until the work we have plays out, then go after him."

Gyp threw back his head and laughed. "Who says we're voting, or that I'm inviting you along?"

Hugh flashed an arrogant grin. "Aren't you the one who said the three of us are better together than alone?"

Holding up a finger to stave off the increasingly irritated woman down the bar, Gyp moved closer to the Fishers, lowering his voice.

"Priest spoke about six jobs. They're spread out, meaning we'd be riding a good distance between each one. Probably wouldn't get back to Wyoming for months."

"I don't see a problem with that," Harvey said. "We could make enough on those jobs to set ourselves up for years. Another two years and we'll never have to work again. We could buy that ranch we've been talking about."

"Live the good life, Gyp." Hugh clasped him on the shoulder.

Taking the last swallow of his whiskey, Gyp rolled the glass between his fingers. The brothers were right. They brought in big money working for Priest, and he saw no end to the jobs. The three of them were critical to the success, which meant a bigger cut could be coming their way. *Would* be coming to them if Gyp had his way.

"I've got a lovely lady waiting for me, gentlemen."

"So, what do you say?" Hugh asked.

A corner of his mouth twitching, Gyp touched a finger to the brim of his hat. "I'll see you boys for breakfast. Right before we ride to Omaha."

Chapter Five

Austin, Texas

"Do you have any idea who gave you these notes, Mr. Miller?" Beth asked the man for the third time, holding one of the forged bills in her hand. The first two times, he'd wiped sweat from his brow, not meeting her gaze. The last had her suspicions rising.

"I'm sorry, Miss…"

"Agent Cartman."

"Uh, yes. I visited several shops and the bank. The bank teller spotted problems with the note. He showed it to the manager, who sent it off to Washington. Never did get paid back for the ten dollars." Miller lifted his gaze from their table in the restaurant. "Maybe you could talk to him about replacing the funds."

"Sorry. You'll need to deal directly with the manager. Frankly, I wouldn't expect to see the money again. I need a list of the stores you visited on the day the bank noticed the counterfeit bill."

"It could've been another day, Miss…uh, Agent Cartman. I brought money from home that week. Maybe it was given to me on one of my earlier trips to town."

"You're right. But I'm going to focus on the day a month ago when the bank teller identified the forgery."

Picking up his cup, he swallowed the last few drops. Beth signaled the server for two refills before continuing.

"It would be helpful if you could tell me where you went and about what time." She lifted her pencil, hovering it over a piece of paper.

Rubbing his temple, the man rested an arm on the table, clearly uncomfortable and in a hurry to leave. "The general store down the street was first. I usually get there about eight in the morning. After that, I went to the saddlery to have a bridle fixed. I wasn't there more than a few minutes before going to the millinery to pick up a dress my wife had altered. That took me a little longer."

"When did you leave there?" Beth asked, noting he continued to avert his gaze.

"I'm not sure. Maybe nine thirty. I came in here for coffee before going to the bank."

"Time?"

"I don't know. Probably ten o'clock."

"After coffee?"

His gaze darted around the room before lowering to stare into his empty cup. Picking up his napkin, his hand shook as he wiped his brow. The room wasn't that warm, yet his face flushed a blotchy red.

"Mr. Miller?"

"The bank. I went to the bank."

His gaze darted to the door when two men walked inside. Lifting a hand, he tried to hide his face, glancing in the opposite direction.

Beth turned to look at the men who selected a table behind her, both facing Miller. "Do you know them, Mr. Miller?"

Shaking his head, he grabbed his hat. "No, no. I don't know who they are." Standing, he didn't say more before hurrying outside.

Laying down money for their coffee, she stood, memorizing the men's faces before following him.

"Mr. Miller. Wait!"

He paid no attention, increasing his pace before turning between two buildings. Beth followed at a run, her hand delving into a pocket to grip her five shot revolver. She peeked around the corner, seeing Miller turn left at the back of the two buildings.

Lifting her skirt, Beth ran after him. By the time she reached the back of the buildings and turned left, Miller had disappeared. Refusing to give up, she continued on, looking between all the buildings, but he was gone.

It would've bothered her more if she didn't know how to find him. The bank manager had told her Miller was a rancher with a small place not far from Austin. Beth had no doubt he knew the men who'd entered the restaurant, feared them. A connection existed between the three. She just needed to find out how they knew each other.

Returning to the restaurant, Beth wasn't surprised to find them gone. When her gaze lit on their empty table, her eyes widened. One bank note lay on top. Snatching it, she held it up, then grimaced. Legal. Setting it back down, she noticed the server standing close by.

"Do you remember the two men who were at this table?"

"Sure." He grabbed the money, shoving the note into a pocket before picking up the empty cups.

"May I ask their names?"

"I don't *know* them, ma'am. Fact is, I don't think they're from around here. Is there anything else?" Impatience laced his question.

"No. Thank you."

Beth hurried outside, hoping to spot the two men. They were nowhere in sight. She'd lost all three in the course of ten minutes. Miller could be found, unless he decided it best to disappear. From the look of fear on his face, she believed it a viable option.

"Agent Cartman?"

Beth stilled at the familiar voice, hoarse from years of smoking and giving orders. Turning, she stared into the piercing gray eyes of Captain Jacob Jones, leader of the Texas Rangers. Fondly referred to as Cap by his men, and a man she held in great respect.

"Captain Jones. It's good to see you."

Stepping closer, he spotted the bulge in the pocket of her skirt. "How long have you been in town?"

"I arrived on yesterday's stage."

Rubbing his stubbled jaw, Cap's gaze wandered the street, a longtime habit he didn't intend to break. "My guess is you're here about the counterfeit bills."

"News travels fast."

"Not really. The sheriff told me about the bills before the bank manager sent them back east for verification. We expected someone would be sent out. Didn't think it would be you, Beth. Not after the way you disappeared a couple years ago."

The use of her nickname and reference to her time with Chan shouldn't have been unexpected. They'd never spoken of their relationship to the older man, yet he knew. Had figured it out early.

"He's not here."

Straightening, she steeled her features. "I didn't come here to see him."

"That so?"

Moving to a nearby bench, she sat down, motioning to the space beside her. Jones relaxed next to her, stretching his arm across the back.

"Left a year after you took off. I tried to get Evans to stay, but he had plans. It was a dang shame to lose one of my best men."

She fell silent, doing her best to focus on her current assignment. "Yes. A real shame."

Cap didn't wait for her to ask. "Headed north. Decided it was time to hunt down one of his brothers."

"Gabe," she whispered before stopping herself. She cleared her throat, not wanting him to suspect her interest. "Do you know if he found him?"

Stretching out his legs, he shook his head. "Don't rightly know," he lied.

Cap knew where Chan ended up and about his job as a U.S. Marshal. He didn't figure the woman next to him would care. Not after the way she'd disappeared.

"Where are you headed now?"

"I spoke to Mort Miller." She leaned closer, lowering her voice. "A couple men walked into the restaurant and spooked him. Miller took off and I lost him."

Cap drew his legs up. "What'd they look like?"

Beth described them, giving an approximate height and weight. "They dressed like cowboys or ranch hands."

"Could be any of a hundred men in Austin. Anything else you remember?"

She shook her head. "Both had ruddy complexions, as if they spend a good deal of time outside. It's not much."

Standing, Cap held out his hand to help her up. "It's time you had a private meeting with the bank manager."

"I had one with him last night."

"Well, Agent Cartman, I don't believe you asked the right questions."

Omaha, Nebraska

"May I get you anything else, Mr. Priest?"

"Not now." Simon Priest stared into the fireplace, a second brandy in his hand. An open book rested in his lap, spectacles resting on his nose.

He'd slept for over twenty hours after returning from his rescue in Big Pine. It had been close, but he'd kept faith that men would come for him. They'd ridden as far as Cheyenne where his three companions stayed. He split off, heading to Omaha.

The arrest had occurred after an evening of drinking and playing cards. He'd been brooding the entire day, his mood dire and temper short. Being accused of cheating had triggered his infamous temper. He'd always regret the bullet which killed the sheriff. Now he sought solace in his chosen town.

Simon loved his home, books, music, and the infrequent visits to the theater. Quiet, peaceful, the way his life was meant to be. Far different from the man he became when he donned the clothes of a wandering cowboy, moving from one town to another. Each place had been chosen for a reason. Every person he approached selected for their skills. It was a necessary guise, one he couldn't wait to shun when returning home.

"Here are your messages, sir." The man who'd served him the last few years set the letters on the edge of the desk. "May I get you another brandy, sir?"

Simon looked up and shook his head. When the door clicked shut, he closed his eyes, rubbing them with the palms of his hands. Even twenty hours of sleep hadn't relieved the nagging weariness plaguing him the last few months.

No matter how far he traveled or the accomplishments he made, nothing brought meaning to his life. He had money, status, a wonderful home, and loyal servants. None of this gave Simon the satisfaction he desired.

He should be going over the details of the next step in the plan. Glancing at the stack of mail on his desk, Simon wondered which envelope included the instructions for his next trip. He couldn't bring himself to care.

Standing, he picked up his glass, eschewing brandy for whiskey. He didn't often mix his drinks, but tonight he needed something more powerful, more pungent.

The woman he'd been seeing had traveled to Kansas City, planning to return in a month. By then, he'd be gone. Simon enjoyed her company, appreciated her wit and intelligence. Tall with curves he could sink his hands into, she'd kept his interest longer than any woman he'd known in a long time. A widow of means, she held little desire to form a lifetime alliance with any man, not even Simon, who she'd been seeing for almost two years.

By now, he'd thought to be married with several children, living off investments. The dream seemed more remote than ever.

Tossing back his drink, wincing at the burning sensation flowing down his throat, Simon filled the glass again. If he were ever to achieve his vision of the future, he'd have to focus his attention on a more suitable partner.

It wouldn't be difficult. Simon knew the single women in Omaha considered him quite eligible. He'd have to be blind not to notice the sideways glances when strolling through town.

Sipping the whiskey, a small smile tipped up his mouth. He would view it as a hunt, searching out the most proper women for his needs, selecting one to pursue. Someone who would ask few questions, be the ultimate hostess, caring wife and mother.

The thought provided more appeal than Simon expected, eliciting a wave of unbidden excitement. It felt good. More than good after all these months of sinking spirits and a sense of dejection.

Could the answer to his hollow life be as simple as meeting a woman who shared his desire for marriage and children? It seemed such a simple solution. Simon wondered how he'd never thought of it before.

Setting down his glass, a sense of renewed passion carried him upstairs and into his bedroom. Tomorrow, he'd start again, creating a new beginning. For the first time in months, he found himself looking forward to the morning.

Chapter Six

Splendor

Chan sat with Gabe, Lena, and their son, Jack, in the second row of the church. Olivia Barnett and Doctor Clay McCord stood with Reverend Paige, saying their vows after a long courtship made necessary by Nick Barnett's stubborn attitude about his daughter marrying.

The couple had planned to marry a couple weeks after Dom Lucero married Josephine Dubois. The tragic death of a young woman during their reception changed their plans, pushing the date a couple months into the future.

"They're quite a handsome couple, don't you think?" Lena asked Chan, not expecting an answer. "Nick can be so stubborn. I'm so glad to see them finally going forward with the wedding."

He glanced at her, then over her head at Gabe, who shrugged. A tenacious businesswoman who'd made her fortune working in partnership with Nick Barnett, she had a soft heart and generous nature.

More than once, she and Nick had words about his obstinate stance about Clay. He liked the man, respected his work, and believed he'd be a good husband to Olivia. Until a few months ago, the fact Clay hadn't pushed harder for Nick's approval frustrated him. One night he'd shown up on the porch with a bottle of whiskey in his hand and his gunbelt around his waist. Something Clay almost never wore.

The doctor had told Nick either he accept the fact Olivia would be his wife, then share the whiskey, or Clay would be taking her from the house at gunpoint. The calm declaration stunned Nick before he threw back his head and laughed. The two men had come to an understanding, finishing the bottle before passing out in Nick's study.

Chan watched Olivia and Clay exchange their vows. He'd been to few weddings since leaving New York, and those he'd attended because the men were fellow Texas Rangers. As a rule, he stayed away from church, uncomfortable with how he felt about God, heaven, and the afterlife.

He'd gone with Lena, Gabe, and their father to Sunday service a few times, but only because he was already at their home. Chan wondered if that was why Lena so often extended him an invitation to supper on Saturday nights. She knew he, Gabe, and Walter would retreat to the study after eating, sharing drinks and stories. Most times, he'd spend the night rather than return to the Lucero ranch. Lena meant well, and he didn't know how to explain his aversion to church, so he remained silent.

Following the couple outside, the procession moved to the Eagle's Nest Restaurant in the St. James Hotel. The chef, Gary Werth, and his assistant, May Covington, Caleb's wife, had prepared a magnificent feast.

Baron Klaussner generously provided venison, pheasant, and wild turkey from his numerous hunts. Dax and Luke Pelletier delivered freshly cut beef, and a group of church ladies donated pies and punch. May, who also served as the restaurant's pastry chef, brought in tray after tray of luscious sweets. Nick, Lena, and Gabe gifted liquor and beer, as well as funding the remainder of the reception.

"You here for a while?"

Chan turned at Beau Davis's voice. One of the deputies who'd been with Gabe the longest, he held out his hand to clasp Beau's.

"No orders yet. I'd prefer to stay on the Lucero ranch for a while, but will go where I'm needed."

He enjoyed both jobs. His desire to spend more time on the ranch surprised Chan, who'd begun thinking about buying a plot of land. A commitment he'd never before considered.

Cash Coulter, Beau's close friend and fellow deputy, joined them, nodding toward the tables laden with food. "Can't recall ever seeing such a fine spread. I suppose we should get in line. Allie won't be happy if I don't get her a big portion of wild turkey and some of May's pastries." He nodded across the room at a table where Allie, Beau's wife, Caro, May's husband, Caleb, and Mack Mackey and his wife, Sylvia, sat.

Glancing at the window as he followed Beau and Cash toward the food, Chan stopped, spotting a familiar looking man. Someone he never thought to see again.

Dressed as any ranch hand, what set him apart were the twin guns strapped around his waist.

Their gazes met, the man's cold, empty eyes holding Chan's. A ball of ice formed in his gut, body tensing. No matter the clothes, Chan knew the man had come for him.

"Chan?"

He shot a distracted look at Beau. "I'll join you in a minute."

Hurrying out the front doors of the hotel, Chan rested his hand on the handle of his six-shooter, his gaze moving up and down the street. He'd lost him.

Bounding down the steps, he moved left toward the other end of town. Splendor had grown significantly over the last two years. Shops, houses, saloons, and a second boardinghouse had been added on streets not existing the first years. It made finding one person more difficult, but not impossible.

Checking each business as he passed by, Chan canvassed another street, then the next. The man seemed to have disappeared, along with the midnight black stallion he always rode. Other than Chinatown, many stores were closed, the owners attending the wedding and reception.

Returning to the main street, he spotted a lone figure sitting outside the jail, a book in his lap. Enoch Weaver had become a figure of great interest since helping to save May from a man planning to gun her and Caleb down.

Considered the town drunk, Gabe had told Chan he'd stepped out of the stagecoach over a year before and never left. Since stepping between May and the gunslinger, people had granted him a small measure of respect.

Over time, Caleb had become a friend of sorts, learning some of Enoch's history. An educated man who spent hours reading, he'd left his prominent position as an attorney in Cincinnati after the tragic deaths of his wife and son. His meals consisted of whatever was in the cupboard of his small cabin on the outskirts of town and whiskey.

Lately, Caleb and May had invited him for supper once a week. Mack and Sylvia Mackey had done what they could to help the older man recover from his intense grief.

"Good afternoon, Enoch." Chan took a seat next to him, not relaxing his guard as he continued to watch for the gunslinger.

Closing the book, Enoch looked up. "Good afternoon, Marshal. I thought you'd be at the reception."

"I had some business to handle. I'll head back in a bit." Movement to his side drew his attention, but it was a man dressed in a suit. "Have you been sitting here long?"

Pulling out his pocket watch, the older man checked the time. "Couple hours. I told the sheriff I'd keep watch so he and the deputies could attend the wedding."

"See much?"

"Quiet a day as we've had in a long time. But that's not why you're asking, is it?"

Chan had forgotten the intelligence hidden under the battered hat and tattered suit. "No, it's not."

Crossing his legs, Enoch clasped his hands on top of the book. "Tell me who caught your attention."

"Cullen Burris. He's wanted for murder."

"Who'd he kill?" Enoch asked.

"A fellow Texas Ranger, a bank manager during a holdup, and a deputy in Austin, Texas. I witnessed him kill the deputy. His brother got between Burris and my bullet. Burris got away. I left the Rangers not long afterward."

"Do you think he's in Splendor?"

"I saw him not half an hour ago standing outside the hotel."

Enoch rubbed his bearded jaw. "Did he see you?"

"Yes."

"I see." Enoch shifted so he could see up and down the street with little effort. "Describe Burris to me."

"Under six feet tall, heavyset, with broad hands. Dressed as a ranch hand, a pair of six-shooters at his waist. Brown hat and boots. Rides a midnight black stallion."

"I saw him ride in early this morning."

Chan sat up. "You're sure?"

"I was eating breakfast at McCall's when he rode past on the horse you described."

"Did you see where he went?"

Enoch shook his head. "He rode toward the other end of town. Did you check Noah's livery?"

"The stallion isn't there."

"Maybe Burris has disappeared. Rode out when he saw you."

A grim smile formed on Chan's face. "Doubtful."

"I agree. Which means he came here for you, Marshal." Enoch continued when Chan didn't respond. "Was his brother a gunslinger, too?"

"No. An accountant and an innocent bystander. He stepped in front of the bullet meant for Cullen."

"Which means he *wasn't* an innocent bystander, Marshal. Assuming you identified yourself."

"I did. Cullen drew his weapon when he saw my badge. I drew mine. His brother walked right in front of him."

"His fault. Not yours. But as with all men who choose an outlaw life, Burris wouldn't have seen it that way. How long ago did this happen?"

"About three years." Chan knew because a few months later, Beth had arrived in Austin, altering his comfortable life.

Enoch stretched out his legs, crossing them at the ankles. "Took him long enough to find you."

Chan couldn't help the chuckle. "Guess so." Standing, he adjusted his hat. "I'd better get back to the reception."

"Are you going to tell your brother about Burris?"

"It seems best."

Enoch drew his legs back under him and opened the book. "I'll watch for him. You be careful."

"I'm always careful, Enoch."

Raising his head, the older man pierced him with a knowing look. "Don't take any chances. Burris rode a long way over treacherous trails to find you. His purpose is clear. There's only one reason he's in Splendor, and that's to kill you."

Chapter Seven

Beth stared out the window of the stage, doing her best not to choke on the swirling dust plaguing her the entire trip. The journey to Kansas City had been agony from the time she boarded the stage in Austin.

There'd been three people traveling with her until Dallas, where they departed and five people filled the stage. All were headed to Kansas City, a long, arduous trip through Indian country.

Captain Jones had given her much to think about, making sure she interviewed everyone who'd mentioned fake bills. No two people received it from the same shop.

An unexpected storm passed over Austin, delaying their trip to the Miller ranch. By the time they arrived, Mort and his wife were gone. Packed what they could in a wagon and disappeared. Because of the lack of tracks, Jones believed Miller hadn't waited to leave. He'd left his ranch and ridden out of Austin the same day.

His departure told Beth a great deal. Miller wasn't innocent. He was a coney dealer, a trader who made money from passing forged bills. She had no idea what middle level position he held in the ring, but Beth was certain he was part of a professional group of counterfeiters.

"Are you traveling alone, dear?"

Beth pulled her gaze from the outside. She guessed the elderly woman beside her to be at least sixty, with a frail frame and skin almost translucent, rather than the leathery look of so many women who'd spent years in the frontier.

"Yes, ma'am. And you?"

The woman chuckled while fiddling with an embroidered handkerchief bunched in her hands. "I've been traveling alone since my husband passed several years ago. He had an insurance business in Chicago."

"What brings you this far south?"

"Our son moved to Austin when he married. He's an attorney." The smile on the woman's face spoke of her pride. "I live in Kansas City now."

"Why not Austin?"

"I have a sister in Kansas City. Besides, Texas is too hot for me. It's better for me to visit every few months. I must say, the dust on this trip is the worst I've experienced."

Beth waved a hand in the air to demonstrate her displeasure. "It is quite awful."

"Do you have family in Kansas City, dear?"

She thought of Thaddeus. He'd left for St. Louis the same time she headed for Austin, following a similar lead. They planned to meet in Kansas City, then continue to follow the money.

"A friend who works with me."

The elderly woman shifted toward her. "Oh, that's wonderful. What type of work?"

Beth glanced at the other passengers. All eyes were closed as if they slept. "I work for the government."

The woman's face brightened. "How interesting."

"Not really. Most days all I do is take care of paperwork and keep my boss's schedule. Nothing exciting." She used her standard reply to queries about her work.

"But you get to travel. That's more than most women do in the jobs open to them."

Beth was aware of the few options open to women, especially the farther west you lived. The bigger towns offered secretarial positions in private business and for the government. Hospitals and schools provided better opportunities than washing laundry or working in seedy saloons.

"Not often, but I'm grateful for what I have." Another statement she'd perfected over the years.

They fell silent as the coach bumped along, Beth closing her eyes to stem the dust while the woman pressed the handkerchief to her face. Before long, the woman's arm dropped to her lap, eyes closed in sleep. The movement caught Beth's attention. She wished to do the same, but experience told her it would be impossible.

Her job required a good deal of travel. Usually by carriage, horseback, or railcar, as most assignments were along the East Coast. Stagecoaches were used when traveling to most destinations west, south, and north of Kansas City.

Closing her eyes again, Beth thought of Mort Miller. Instinct told her the rancher was a link in the forgery ring. The weather had slowed her progress, allowing him to get away. Captain Jones assured her he and the sheriff would contact lawmen in Texas and nearby states with Miller's description and suspected crime. Perhaps he'd already be in custody by the time she arrived in Kansas City. She grinned at the fantasy.

Busting counterfeiting operations took long hours of analyzing clues, months of following leads, and countless time spent interviewing those suspected of being involved. Oftentimes, those who ended up with fake bills knew more than they first thought.

Legislation permitting only the federal government and chartered national banks to print money had helped, cutting down on forgeries during the Civil War. New laws had never stopped enterprising criminals, and the same held true for talented coney men. The good ones always found a way to get around whatever the government did to stop them.

Those were the individuals who kept her, Thaddeus, and other agents from seeking other employment. As long as there were those who chose to live outside the law, there'd be a need for agencies such as the Secret Service, Texas Rangers, and other law enforcement agencies.

People like Thaddeus, herself, and Captain Jones. And men such as Chan Evans.

"You've seen no forgeries being passed?" Thaddeus set down more of the fake bills, a brow arching when his gaze moved up to meet the sheriff's.

"Not like these." He pointed at the ones Thaddeus handed him before pulling bills from a drawer in his desk. "This is what several bank managers have brought in over the last few weeks." The sheriff slid them toward Thaddeus. "All from a national bank in the Montana Territory. Tens and ones. I sent one of each denomination to Washington, but haven't heard back. I've got a box full of them."

Reaching down to the last drawer, he grasped a box, setting it on the desk. Opening the top, exposing dozens of bills, he slid it across the desk.

Selecting a couple, Thaddeus held them up. "These are good. Excellent, actually. You say they're all from the same bank?" He turned the notes over. "National Bank of Big Pine, Montana. Did you send a telegram to the bank manager?"

"No. I was waiting for word from Washington to confirm they're forgeries."

He selected a few more, studying each one. "They're forgeries, Sheriff."

Reaching out, the lawman picked one from the box. "You're certain?"

"This is all I do. Study fake bills and hunt down the people who put them into circulation. These are forgeries, Sheriff. No doubt in my mind. Do you mind if I keep a couple?"

"If they'll help you locate who's passing the bogus notes, not at all."

Thaddeus tucked them into a pocket, then leaned back. "Do you have names of the people who brought them into the banks?"

"Right here." The sheriff handed him a piece of paper. "I spoke to each one, and to the people they believed gave them the fake money."

"And they swore they had no idea the bills weren't real." He didn't try to temper his sarcasm. "The best coney dealers are superb liars. I'll wager most of those who took the money to banks are innocent victims. It's the ones who gave them the money we have to talk to again."

Wincing, the sheriff shook his head. "I've tried to keep track of them. Most have disappeared."

"What about families?"

"Disappeared."

"Friends?" Thaddeus asked.

"Not that anyone wants to admit. I identified four. Three men and a woman. I've got their names, but they're probably aliases. Interesting, though."

"What?"

"One of the men has a son about six. He was with his father when we talked. The boy made a comment about being from Montana."

Thaddeus's brows rose. "Big Pine?"

"He didn't say before his father told him to be quiet and get to his room. There is something else, though."

"What?"

"When the postmaster heard about the forgeries, he came to talk to me. Said he remembered delivering packages to a couple of the people I interviewed."

Thaddeus leaned forward, resting his arms on the desk. "Did he remember where the packages came from?"

"Sure did. A place called Splendor, Montana."

"Kansas City up ahead!"

The driver's loud shout brought everyone to attention. It had been days since they'd left Dallas, with occasional stops at desolate outposts to take care of personal needs and eat.

The land had been rougher than Beth remembered from one other trip from Austin to Kansas City. She hadn't been in the best of moods during that journey, so perhaps her memory was flawed. Regardless, she ached all over, her backside numb, stomach grumbling for decent food.

"Do you have someone to meet you?"

Beth gave a quick nod of her head at the older woman's question. "Yes, I do. What about you?"

"My sister and her husband will be there with a buggy. I do the same when they travel to see their children. It is nice having family close by."

Beth wouldn't know. Her father died within a year of Abner's death. Her mother chose to stay in the home her husband had built in upper New York after retiring from a lifetime of government work. Beth tried to visit a couple times a year, but with her job and changing schedule, it had become more difficult as each year passed.

Leaning out the window, she felt a wave of relief at the approaching town. Beth recalled the growing town had a population of over thirty thousand, which meant there'd be decent hotels and restaurants. After meeting Thaddeus, a hot bath, clean clothes, and a large meal were her priorities.

Brushing hair from her eyes, she leaned down to pick up the small satchel at her feet. It held her most important items, including extra ammunition for her .32 caliber pocket revolver, a change of clothes, and hairbrush. The rest of her possessions were in the larger satchel on top of the stage.

Letting out a grateful breath when the stage pulled to a stop, she sat up, ready for the door to open. A moment later, it did.

"It was a pleasure talking with you."

"Same here, dear." The older woman touched Beth's arm, squeezing. "Take good care of yourself."

Smiling at her, Beth ducked enough so as not to hit her head on the door's frame and stepped to the ground. She glanced around, slightly frustrated at not seeing Thaddeus.

Waiting as the driver and guard handed down the luggage for those leaving the stage, she gripped her small bag, tugging the large one to the boardwalk and straightening.

"Beth!"

Whirling around, she relaxed at the sight of Thaddeus hurrying up to her. "I'm exhausted. Tell me you have a hotel with a hot bath ready for me."

An apologetic look crossed his face as he reached down to grab her larger satchel. "Sorry, Beth. You have just enough time to eat before we board the train."

The image of a cleansing bath and hot meal dissolved. "Train?"

"I've gotten an excellent lead on where the forgers might be staying."

Her shoulders slumped. She wanted to catch them as much as Thaddeus, but she also needed to take care of her basic needs. Resigned, she met his gaze.

"All right. Where are we going?"

"Splendor, a small town in the Montana Territory."

Chapter Eight

Lucero Ranch

"I sure would've liked to have been there to see Sterling's face when they blew up his jail." Curly leaned back in his saddle, cackling. "Bet he was spitting mad."

Chan couldn't stop his grin. "That he was."

"And he ain't going to forget what they did. You mark my words, Marshal. He'll be after that Priest fella like a rabid dog."

"I doubt he'll give up his position to follow him, Curly. The fact is I got a telegram from him yesterday. Judge Collins wants to see me in Big Pine next week."

"Another trial?"

"Sterling didn't say."

"A man of few words." Curly cackled again. "When we rode together, days would go by without him uttering more than a few words. Good thing I learned to read his mind." He pointed at the herd up ahead. "Guess I'd best get those strays. You stay here."

Chan watched him ride off, thinking about why the judge would want to see him if there wasn't a trial. Maybe he wanted to form another posse to go after Priest and his men. A foolish notion as they could be in Mexico by now, or circled back up into Canada. His guess was they'd split up, scattering across a few states.

What of the other Priest, the one Gabe heard about during the war? Were he and Simon related? Was that where Simon would've gone, or did he have his own hideout?

None of those answered the question of why Collins wanted to see him. For the first time since becoming a U.S. Marshal, Chan felt a rush of unease.

He could handle the unknown, had done it many times in his life. Chan knew how to take orders, which was what his job entailed.

This was a different kind of unease, not caused by fear or a sense of dread. More of a restless disquiet.

"Those damn animals don't want to behave." Curly reined next to him.

Their job today was to guard the herd and round up strays. Another typical day on the Lucero ranch when they weren't moving cattle from one pasture to another. An easy job compared to most ranch work. The work gave Chan time to think, something he'd done too little of since coming to Splendor.

"When are you gonna ride out, Marshal?"

"I've got a couple days yet. Why?"

"I'm thinking I may go with you. Haven't seen Sterling's scrawny hide in a long time. Maybe I can talk him into retiring and moving this way."

Shoving his hat off his forehead, Chan's mouth twisted into a grin. "Are you sure you want to have him so close by? He can be an ornery cuss."

"Don't I know it. But I've got this burning in my gut that his time is short as the sheriff. Too many varmints out there, and his reflexes ain't as good as when he was a young'un."

Chan couldn't argue that. He didn't know how old Sterling was, but he had to be in his late fifties, the same as Curly.

"He'd be a hard man to replace," Chan said.

"That he would. Still, it's time someone younger took over. Not you, Marshal. You enjoy ranching too much to give it up."

"How would you know that?"

"It ain't hard. You've got this look on your face when working the cattle. You're smart, and if I were a guessing man, I'd say you probably got enough stowed away to start your own ranch."

Chan didn't respond. He'd been thinking the same, but there were still things he wanted to do before settling down for good, which a ranch would require. Right now, he enjoyed both jobs, although he found himself wanting longer stretches of time at the ranch between assignments.

A shout had both men turning to look behind them, waving when they recognized the rider. Bull Mason, one of two foremen at the Pelletier ranch, joined them a minute later, holding out a piece of paper.

"Good to see you, boys. Got a message for you from Rachel and Ginny." He handed it over, mentioning Dax's and Luke's wives.

"What do those women have planned now?" Chan took the paper, reading the short invitation, handing it to Curly, whose nose wrinkled.

"I ain't available," he said, giving the note back to Chan. "Perfect for you, though."

Bull shifted in the saddle, chuckling. "They swear it's nothing more than a way to introduce Rachel's friends to the locals. This is going out to singles and married couples. It's on a Sunday, so most people can come. Food, music, and you don't have to stay long. Would you let Dom, Josie, and Mal know about it?"

"Sure can." Chan tucked it into a pocket. "Do you want me to tell Gabe and Lena?"

"Dirk's riding into town to pass the word. Anyone who can come is invited. How's your herd doing?"

"The longhorns are doing good. We'll know more when the cold sets in and there's snow. What about the ones you have?" Chan asked.

"Same, but Dax and Luke are optimistic they'll make it through the winter. I should be getting back. See you two on Sunday." Bull reined his horse around, holding up a hand in farewell as he rode off.

"I ain't going to no shindig introducing a bunch of single women. I'll leave that to you and the other bachelors."

"It's an excuse to get off the ranch for a few hours, Curly."

"Don't care. I'm happy right here."

Chan knew once the man made up his mind, there'd be no changing it. "I'll give them your regrets."

"What's that?"

Chan hid his grin. "Never mind. I'll tell them you volunteered to stay with the herd. If Dom doesn't have anyone else willing to help, I'll keep you company."

"Hell, I can watch the cattle with one arm tied behind me. You go on and have a good time. Besides, I'll enjoy the quiet."

Two days later, Chan understood what Curly meant about enjoying the quiet. There were at least three hundred people at the Pelletier ranch. Which sounded like most of the town, except Splendor had grown to over three thousand.

Most of the single men were in attendance. No surprise, as there was a shortage of eligible women in the territory. Rachel's friends had come all the way from the East Coast at her invitation. Two nurses she'd served with during the war, both a little younger than her. Two more were teachers, and one educated as a lawyer. All pretty in their own ways and single.

Chan stood on the sidelines with the married men, watching their wives refill platters of food and replenish the punch bowl. He watched the men whirl the new arrivals around the makeshift dance floor, laughing as they flew by.

Every once in a while, Caleb, Mack, and the other married men would grab their wives for a dance. Mostly, they enjoyed the food while watching the entertainment in front of them.

"You should be out there, Chan." Gabe's hand clasped his shoulder.

"I'm considering it."

"Have you even met them?"

"I introduced myself. Seems their dance cards are already full."

"Doesn't stop you from talking to them," Gabe said.

Chan studied the women. Two appeared interested in him. One of the nurses and the attorney. Even so, he couldn't summon the energy to pursue either of them.

"Do they all have jobs?" Chan asked.

"The nurses will work a few hours a week at the clinic. Clay and Doc Worthington expect they'll be full-time soon. Dirk's wife, Rosemary, is expecting, so she won't be available at the clinic as much." Gabe nodded toward the lawyer. "The attorney plans to open an office. Noah and Abby Brandt plan to give her some of their business."

"What about the two teachers?"

"One will be helping in the Eagle's Nest kitchen, and the other is going to help Suzanne at the boardinghouse. We're hoping they all stay." Gabe lifted his hand in greeting to a ranching family from south of Splendor.

Chan didn't see an issue with them staying. Not with the interest shown by the single men.

Gabe nudged his shoulder. "Over there. The lawyer isn't dancing. Why don't you head over?"

How could Chan tell his brother only one woman appealed to him, and she was hundreds of miles away in New York? He'd been quiet about what happened between him and Beth, never mentioning the agent who'd walked out on him without explanation. Which was why he needed to move on, as she had.

"Why not?" Handing Gabe his glass, Chan made his way across the expanse to where the woman stood talking with Ginny Pelletier.

Her deep, throaty laugh wafted through the air. Uninhibited and unpretentious, as were her clothes and hair. Pretty without making a fuss about her appearance.

Chan winced. *What was her name?*

"Oh, Francesca. I do like you." Ginny laughed again, swiping a tear from her face.

Francesca. Right. Chan continued forward, stopping in front of them. "Ladies."

"Hello, Chan. Have you met Francesca O'Reilly? She's an attorney from New York."

His gaze latched onto the newcomer. "We met when I first arrived. Do you dance, Miss O'Reilly?"

"I've been known to, Mr. Evans."

Chan was surprised she remembered his last name. He held out his hand. "Care to honor me with a dance?"

Taking his hand, he led her onto the dance floor for a waltz. Chan knew his dancing skills were excellent, having been tutored since a young boy. He shouldn't have been surprised when Francesca matched him step for step.

"You dance very well, Mr. Evans. Or should I call you Marshal Evans?"

"I'd prefer if you call me Chan."

"Then you'll call me Francesca." She smiled up at him, and for the first time in two years, his stomach flipped.

Chan didn't want it to, had no desire to feel anything for this woman other than friendship. He told himself it was because he hadn't been with a woman in a long time, nor attempted to meet anyone.

"Francesca. Italian, right?"

"Yes. Half Italian and half Irish. So watch yourself. I'm known to have a fierce temper."

Laughing, Chan relaxed, feeling a sense of peace which had evaded him for too long. When the waltz ended and a polka began, he arched a brow, silently requesting a second dance.

"I love the polka," she answered, proving it by executing the jaunty dance with skill.

By the time the guests began to leave, they'd danced several more times, shared punch and stories about growing up in New York. He'd also spent time with two more of the single women, dancing with each.

But it was Francesca he made a point of saying goodbye to, and who held his thoughts during the ride back to Dom's ranch. Even if he wasn't ready to request anything more, it felt good to laugh and relax.

Chan couldn't help thinking he'd reached a point where he could tuck Beth into his past and begin the process of seeking a different future.

75

Chapter Nine

Chan rode the trail to Big Pine, watching for any signs of the renegade Crow band. Sightings had become less frequent, as had the raids.

The last major one occurred when Dom's father and brother drove a herd of longhorns to Montana from Texas. There'd been no deaths, but both Dom and Josie had been wounded.

Continuing his vigil, Chan once again wondered about the reason for his summons to Big Pine. Judge Collins always made it a point to give detailed information with each request. This time had been an exception.

If Sterling had somehow tracked Priest down, the sheriff would've let him know. Which meant there was another reason for the trip. He thought of Curly's comment, his grip on the reins tightening.

What if Sterling meant to retire and the judge offered Chan the sheriff's job? Unlike when Dom mentioned taking on the job as marshal, he felt no rush of anticipation at the possibility of becoming Big Pine's next sheriff.

Knowing he'd discover the judge's reason in a few hours, Chan forced his mind to other topics. The Pelletiers had a parcel of land they weren't using north of Dom's ranch. It was about two hours from Splendor and was closer to the Blackfoot camp than any of the other ranches. The benefits were great.

Almost a thousand acres of rich pasture, two streams on the property, and Wildfire Creek on the west boundary. Redemption's Edge was on the southwest side, the Lucero ranch on the southeast.

By Montana standards, a thousand acres wasn't much. For Chan, it would mean setting down roots, a move he wasn't ready for quite yet. After a discussion with Dax and Luke, they'd promised to let him know if anyone else expressed an interest. An agreement which suited Chan fine.

Relaxing, he allowed himself to forget the inherent dangers between Splendor and Big Pine. His last few trips had been uneventful. No sign of the Crow renegades for months. Which was why the shots and angry shouts behind him caught Chan unaware.

Leaning over the saddlehorn, he drew the gun from its holster and glanced behind him. A small party of three Crow approached from about a hundred yards back. Each held a rifle aimed at him.

He kicked Caesar into a gallop, forcing himself to control his breathing before turning and firing. It would be almost impossible to hit them at this distance with a six-shooter, but the effort might slow them down.

Big Pine wasn't that far ahead. A few miles at most. If he could make it close to the town limits, he had a good chance of them giving up.

Another shot whizzed past. He bent lower, giving them a smaller target. As he reached behind to get off his own shot, a bullet ripped through his shirt. The sting didn't come for several seconds, enough time for him to raise his gun and take two shots of his own.

Chan didn't know how, but one bullet knocked a rider off his horse, the others slowing and stopping, whooping even as they slid to the ground to help their fallen comrade.

Not waiting to see if they'd resume the pursuit, Chan gave Caesar his head, the gelding galloping as fast as it could go. The buildings of the territorial capital came into view. The pain in his arm increased even as relief flooded through him.

Chan glanced at his bloodied shirt, smirking at the thought he'd been hurt much worse. He didn't feel the wooziness or the hard ground as he tumbled onto it.

Big Pine

"You'll be sore for a while, but otherwise, the wound will heal fine, Marshal. This wasn't just a graze. It tore right through your arm. That's why there was so much blood and you passed out. I suspect telling you to take it easy for a few days won't do any good."

Chan slid off the table and stood. "You'd be right, Doc." Taking the few steps to a row of hooks on the wall, he grabbed his gunbelt, wincing in pain as he secured it around his waist. Settling his hat on his head, he turned. "Who found me?"

All he remembered was thinking what a slight wound he'd received before feeling himself plummet to the ground. He didn't even know how much time passed before he woke in the Big Pine clinic.

"Stagecoach from Splendor. The driver recognized your buckskin gelding. He told Sheriff Sterling you were a dozen feet away under a tree. The man said it looked like your horse dragged you there." The doctor chuckled, handing Chan a bottle of laudanum. "Take this for pain."

Shaking his head, he waved the addictive pain killer away. "Give it to someone who needs it, Doc."

He set the bottle on a shelf. "Stubborn as most men I know. That hard head will get you killed someday, Marshal."

Chan didn't doubt it. His mother and father had told him the same.

"Sterling says to come to the jail when you're up to it. He told me to tell you your horse is at the livery and he got a room for you at the Imperial Hotel. I suppose you're going to head to the jail instead of the hotel to rest."

Shooting the doctor a brash grin, Chan reached into his pocket, pulling out some bills. "Here's for your services. Thanks, Doc."

"You take care of yourself."

Stepping into the waning evening light, he took a slow look around. The clinic had two stories and was located on a back street. Larger than the one in Splendor, he'd counted two doctors, three nurses, and several examination rooms on the ground floor.

Stepping off the boardwalk, he crossed the street. His stomach growled. He should stop for supper, but his curiosity over the reason for his summons to Big Pine gnawed at him.

The doc was wrong. He headed into the hotel long enough to change his shirt, but not rest. Getting that accomplished, Chan returned to the boardwalk, rubbing his left arm in an unconscious gesture to relieve the pain.

Passing several businesses, he made a quick stop at the livery. Caesar had been groomed and fed. He saw no signs of injury or lacerations from a rifle shot. Satisfied, he continued to the jail, the energy he'd felt at the clinic beginning to fade. Pace slowing, he stopped for a minute to rub his arm again, releasing a tired breath.

Chan told himself he'd suffered worse. Somehow it didn't matter when another jolt of pain shot through his arm, spreading to his shoulder and down his side. He thought of returning to the clinic for the laudanum, dismissing the idea on a curse.

Reaching the door of the jail, he shoved it open, stepped inside, and froze. Occupying a chair across the desk from Sterling sat Agent Elizabeth Cartman.

Beth, the woman who'd haunted him for two years, met his gaze, cool, assessing, and except for a momentary twitch at the corners of her eyes, unemotional. Her expression left no doubt she expected him. He wished Sterling had taken the time to warn him, but knowing Beth, she hadn't revealed their prior association. Chan refused to give their time together the significance of a *relationship*.

"How's your arm?" Sterling asked.

"Fine." His gaze didn't stray from Beth's.

"Marshal Evans, this is—"

"Agent Cartman," Chan interrupted, his voice distant, professional, and cold as a Montana winter. "What brings you to Big Pine?"

Sterling looked between them, clearing his throat as Chan grabbed a chair. Swinging it around, he straddled it, resting his arms on the back, ignoring the slice of pain.

"She's here with her partner, Agent Thaddeus Taylor." The sheriff nodded across the room.

A slender man of average height, dark hair graying at the temples, and mustache peppered with silver stood by the stove, a tin cup in his hand. Walking forward, he held out his hand.

"Thad Taylor."

Standing, he grasped the outstretched hand, glad the bullet hadn't struck his right arm. "Chan Evans."

"The U.S. Marshal Sheriff Sterling holds in such high esteem," the agent said.

Dropping Thad's hand, he stopped himself from sending a confused glance at Sterling. "Are you the reason Judge Collins called me here?" Chan sat back down, not sparing Beth a glance.

"We are." Thad picked up a chair from against the wall and sat down. "We've been following the trail of counterfeiters. Our latest information indicates the source may be located in this area."

"Big Pine?" Chan asked.

"And perhaps Splendor."

"You think there's a coney man in Splendor?" Neither his expression nor his voice changed. Inwardly, the news stunned him. "Getting the equipment across the country would be expensive and difficult. I understand artists, engravers, even dealers being in remote locations, but printers? It doesn't make sense to me. I'd expect them to be in places such as St. Louis, Kansas City, or New Orleans. Or any of the large cities back east."

"That's why we're here, Marshal. We need to figure out if the information we have is accurate or another false lead. They could be located right here in Big Pine, which in my mind, makes more sense."

Chan continued to focus on Thad, ignoring Beth a few feet away, her posture rigid, expression bland. "What do you want from me? I know nothing about counterfeiting."

"You know both towns, the area, the people. Agent Cartman says you have excellent instincts and a quick mind."

Sheriff Sterling again glanced between them, but remained silent. Chan knew he'd have some explaining to do.

"Did you know I was the marshal up here?"

Thad shook his head. "No. When the sheriff mentioned you, Beth reminded me about the assignment in Austin and how you were instrumental in locating and arresting the bank robbers. She had great respect for you."

Chan couldn't hold back a disbelieving snort. "That was because we were hunting men I'd already tracked to a hideout in Texas. I understand bank robbers, murderers, and thieves. Coney men are beyond my expertise. I'd suggest you work with Sheriff Sterling and Sheriff Gabe Evans in Splendor."

He noticed Beth's eyes widen for an instant before her features stilled. Chan had mentioned his oldest brother, as well as his desire to locate Gabe, several times during their brief time together. He was surprised she remembered.

Thad sent an uneasy glance at Beth. "We'd prefer to work with you, Marshal."

Standing, Chan turned the chair around, resting his hand on the back. "I've got plenty to do already. I'm afraid you'll need to find someone else." He thought of the gunman he'd seen in Splendor, feeling an urgency to return home.

"You'll get paid for your time, Marshal," Thad said.

"Money means nothing to me, Agent Taylor. When I'm not handling work as a marshal, I work a ranch north of Splendor. The owner needs me there, and frankly, that appeals to me much more than working on this case." He held out his hand, which Thad gripped after a brief hesitation. "Good luck."

Nodding at Sterling, he left, his gaze never once connecting with Beth's. Stepping outside, Chan exhaled an unsteady breath before taking purposeful steps down the street.

Seeing Beth had shaken him, the gut punch at her presence not receding while he spoke with Thad. She looked good. Better than good. She couldn't have been more beautiful if she wore a silk evening gown instead of the plain, brown dress and boots.

Somewhere in the yards of fabric he knew a gun would be hidden. He wondered if she still wore the twin six-shooters, although he saw no evidence of them around her still tiny waist. The memory brought another slice of pain. This time, though, it wasn't to his arm.

The assignment interested him. The people he'd have to work with held no appeal.

It would be better for them to work with the sheriffs. They knew their towns and the people better than Chan, and there'd be no issues regarding unresolved history. A history he had no intention of revisiting.

Chapter Ten

"Do you want to tell me what exactly went on between you and Evans?" Standing in the largest room at the Imperial Hotel, Thad poured two drinks, handing a glass to Beth.

He'd requested a suite. What he'd gotten was an oversized bedroom with sitting area, small desk, and settee. The decanter of brandy and glasses were an added benefit, which Thad knew would appear on his bill.

"Don't consider lying to me. I've been with you in meetings many times, and not one man could keep his eyes off you. Evans couldn't stand to look at you."

He sat next to her on the settee, took a sip of his drink, and waited.

Beth stared into her glass, deciding what to say. Thad was Abner's closest friend, his confidant, his occasional partner when searching for some of the most hardened criminals.

"Just say it, Beth."

"Say what, Thad?"

"You're a good agent but a terrible liar. How long were the two of you involved?"

Heat infused her face, throat tightening on Thad's excellent instincts. "I hadn't planned to tell you."

He shrugged, letting her know he'd already figured that out. "Answer my questions."

Rolling the glass between her fingers, she raised it to her lips, emptying it in three swallows. Glancing away, she released a trembling breath.

"You already know how we met."

"During your assignment in Austin."

Nodding, she bit her lower lip, wondering at her hesitancy in admitting what happened. "We became close." She met his steady gaze. "*Very* close."

"You're entitled to a life, Beth. Abner wouldn't have wanted you to shut yourself off from a future." Leaning forward, he rested his arms on his thighs. "Did you walk away or did he?"

She winced at his perception. "I did."

"Then you didn't love him."

"No. I *did* love Chan. Still do. Seeing him today hurt more than I'd ever imagined." She remembered the sharp stab to her chest when he entered the jail. The want and desire she'd tried to hide for far too long.

Cocking his head, he raised a brow. "Then why did you leave?"

"I've asked myself that a thousand times."

"And?"

"I don't have a good answer. Fear, guilt. I'm also older than Chan."

Thad smiled at the disgruntled look on her face. "Do you really believe that mattered to Evans?"

"Not really."

"So what do you plan to do?"

Beth lifted her gaze, brows furrowing. "What do you mean?"

"Evans. We'll be working with him. Will you be able to do your job without letting the past interfere?"

"You heard him. Chan has no desire to work with us. At least with me. It might be better if I returned to Kansas City and followed other leads."

"What other leads?"

Standing, she set her empty glass by the decanter, rubbing her forehead as she paced toward the window. "Surely there must be others who acted as dealers. People who know where the second source is."

"How do you know there's more than one location? So far, we've identified just this one. That's why we're in Big Pine, following the lead," Thad said.

"It doesn't solve the problem about Chan refusing to work with us."

"We'll find a way to change his mind."

Beth chuckled at this. "Chan is the most stubborn man I've ever met. Once he makes up his mind, there is little anyone can do to change it."

Standing, he topped off his glass. "Everyone has a weakness. We just need to find his."

Taking a step closer, she glared at him. "You intend to blackmail him?"

"I'll do whatever it takes to find the source of the forgeries. If the marshal is the man to do this, I *will* find a way to change his mind."

Beth had no doubt Thad would come up with a solution. She just didn't want his scheme to include her.

Chan sat alone at a table in the back of a saloon on the eastern edge of Big Pine. He'd chosen the remote location on purpose. There'd be no chance Beth and Thad would come this far from their hotel, and seeing them again wasn't an option.

Spotting her in the jail had jolted him, the ache real, as if he'd been slammed in the chest with an ax. For an instant, his hands had fisted at his sides before he regained control, hiding his reaction by grabbing a chair. Breathing had been difficult. He'd fought the urge to leave by focusing his attention on Sterling, then Thad.

Ignoring Beth hadn't been easy. There were so many questions begging for answers. Chan had spent two years doing all he could to forget the beguiling agent, only to have her show up unannounced and expecting his help.

Not this time. Never again would he allow himself to be partnered with a woman he no longer trusted.

Tipping his glass, Chan swallowed the whiskey, relishing the slow burn down his throat. The alcohol accomplished two goals—easing the pain in his arm and numbing the memory of Beth. The memory a scant couple hours old.

Shouting and the sound of chairs hitting the floor stopped his morose thoughts. Two men across the room squared off against each other. Chan rocked back in his chair, uninterested in a local brawl over cards. Sheriff Sterling and his deputies were available for such disturbances, leaving him to continue ruminating about the twist of events.

He'd expected a request to hunt down a killer, search for bank robbers, or escort a prisoner to the territorial prison near Deer Lodge. Joining an investigation into forgeries of bank notes never crossed his mind.

Chan had no experience with coney men and their pals acting as dealers, passing the bogus bills around the country. The idea intrigued him, and he would've accepted had it meant working with Thad and Sterling.

A shot rang out through the saloon, his peace shattered. Cursing under his breath, Chan stood, drawing his own weapon. Pointing it at the man who'd fired the gun, he spotted a short, barrel-chested man with a short beard lying on the floor. Blood bloomed from a wound to his shoulder.

"Drop your gun."

The shooter didn't draw his stunned expression away from the man on the floor. Chan saw how his hand shook, color draining from his face.

"*Drop...the...gun,*" Chan repeated, moving closer. In his experience, a scared man could be more unpredictable than a seasoned gunfighter. He moved forward, his gun aimed at the man's chest.

"I didn't mean to shoot him."

Chan got closer. "Hand me your gun."

The man looked at the hand still holding the smoking gun, surprised to see it. Dropping the weapon, he took an unsteady step backward. The instant the six-shooter hit the floor, several men rushed to help the wounded man.

"Someone get the doctor." Continuing to hold his gun on the shooter, Chan bent down, picking up the revolver. "You're coming with me."

The man looked at him as if seeing Chan for the first time. Walking forward on leaden feet, he left the saloon, turning toward the jail.

Beth stood on the balcony of her room, watching the activity on the street below. The second floor of the Imperial Hotel offered a good view of the main street. The jail stood across the street and several buildings to her left.

She'd noticed Sterling had no one in the cells, although the last one appeared to be boarded up from what Beth assumed had been an escape attempt. She found herself wondering if it had been successful.

Resting her arms on the rail, she leaned forward, listening to the sounds of nearby saloons. Beth found herself wondering if Chan had taken a room in the Imperial or one of the many saloons. Or perhaps he'd already left for Splendor. The thought left a hollow ache in her chest.

Seeing him had brought back so many memories, good and bad. They'd argued several times about the best way to bring in bank robbers, laughed at stories of each other's youth, and talked of a future. She'd known Chan had fallen in love with her. He'd voiced his feelings more than once. Beth had never responded, although her feelings were as true as his.

She'd fallen hard. It had all come too fast, too soon after Abner's death. The intensity of her desire had scared Beth, triggered powerful surges of guilt. She hadn't been ready to leave her late husband behind, switch her love to another man.

At the time, leaving seemed the right decision. It was the way she'd severed ties, which had been wrong, hurtful, and cowardly. Beth had seen the disgust in Chan's eyes the instant he'd seen her at the jail. His easy dismissal, focusing all his attention on Thad, had cut deep. In truth, she'd expected nothing less.

The sight of two men, one with a gun trained on the other's back, caught her attention. Even from this distance, she made out Chan's tall figure, determination in the strength of his pace.

Her breath caught, heart raced at the impressive image he made. People stepped aside, moving into the street or crossing it as the two approached. A moment later, they disappeared into the jail.

Thirty minutes passed before Chan stepped outside and stopped. His gaze moved over the street before settling on the Imperial Hotel. Beth's chest squeezed when he spotted her standing on the balcony.

He didn't look away. Instead, his intense stare bored into her. She could feel the revulsion emanating off him. A minute passed before Chan tore his attention from her and left the boardwalk. Following his path, she watched as he ducked out of sight under the balcony, indicating he had a room at the Imperial.

Stepping away from the rail, she returned to her room, closing the door on a soft click. Leaning back against it, she let out a regretful breath. How many times had Beth wished she could go back two years and have a second chance?

From his reaction to seeing her, and the look on his face as he watched her standing on the balcony, any hope she had of rectifying the past wouldn't occur. Any affection he held for her, the love he professed, died the morning she'd left the terse note and disappeared.

A hard knock had Beth taking slow steps to the door, expecting to see Thad. Gripping the knob, she pulled the door open, startled at who stood in the hall. Seconds passed before she found her voice.

Straightening her spine, she blocked Chan's path, indicating he would not be entering her room. "What are you doing here?"

Instead of answering, he stepped forward, resting his hands on her shoulders. Turning her to the side, he walked past.

Placing fisted hands on her hips, she glared at him. "You shouldn't be in here."

Remaining silent, his gaze raked over her, resting on her lush lips. Taking a few steps forward, he stopped inches from her, his silence infuriating.

Beth held her ground, determined to show him his presence didn't bother her. "You need to leave."

She had no time to respond before he grasped the back of her neck with one hand, her waist with the other, and tugged her to him. Warm, firm lips captured hers.

A combination of outrage and passion ripped through her. Slipping her hands between them, she intended to shove him away. Instead, he broke the kiss, setting her aside.

His heated gaze locked on her. "That, Beth, is a *proper* goodbye."

Chapter Eleven

Goodbye.

The word stuck in Beth's throat hours after Chan had walked out. She sat on a chair by the window, wishing he'd never come to her room. But she understood.

He'd wanted to give her a taste of what she'd given him. The tactic worked.

Closing her eyes, she rocked back in the chair. Chan left no doubt there would be no truce, no working together on breaking the forgery ring, and no second chance. It had been a skillful end to any further association.

Beth wondered what Thad would say if she told him about Chan's visit. It was the last thought she had before waking to knocking on the door. Early morning sunlight streamed through the window.

Yawning, she pushed out of the chair. This time, Beth knew it wouldn't be Chan standing in the hall. Drawing the door open, she waved Thad inside.

"You look as if you haven't slept at all."

"Very little. If you give me a few minutes, I'll meet you downstairs for breakfast. I assume you have a plan for going forward with the investigation."

Thad smiled. "I'll meet you downstairs and explain everything."

Closing the door behind him, he bounded down the steps, heading for the dining room. Not waiting for the head server, he selected a table by the window, feeling a wave of exhilaration.

His late meeting the night before had gone better than expected. Beth would be stunned, and Chan...

The pounding of boots on the hardwood floor had a smirk forming on Thad's face. Chan stormed toward him, undisguised anger blazing with every step.

"What the hell did you do, Taylor?" Chan didn't bother to be invited before taking a seat at the table. "You're a real sonofabitch."

"Never denied it, Marshal."

Chan pointed at his badge. "I'll give this up before I let you manipulate me."

"I doubt that. Your pride won't let you give up or disappoint."

"Who the hell would I disappoint?"

Beth drew up short at the shouts coming from the dining room. Recognizing both voices, she gritted her teeth, seething with anger.

"What is going on here?" Her stern, unbending voice had the desired effect. Both men clamped their mouths shut, leaning back in their chairs. Taking a seat, she scooted as far away from Chan as possible. Calmly resting her hands on the table, she looked between them. "I'm ready for an explanation."

"Do you remember when I told you Marshal Evans would be joining us in the investigation?"

She nodded. "What did you do?"

"I fulfilled my promise."

Beth didn't like the triumphant tone of Thad's voice or the incensed look on Chan's chiseled face. "Explain it to me."

"Ah, there you are." The robust voice came from behind them. "Do you mind if I join you?" Judge Collins didn't wait for a response before lowering his rotund frame into a chair. "I didn't like the way you left my house, Marshal. I'm here to offer an explanation."

Chan raised his hand to his badge, removing it from his shirt. "No need, Judge." Setting the badge on the table, he started to stand.

"Sit down, Marshal. You're *not* quitting on me."

"I respect you as much as any man, Judge, but I can quit whenever I want."

Reaching into a pocket, Collins pulled out a telegram, handing it to Chan. "Yes, you can. But I'm hoping you'll change your mind once you've read this."

Unfolding it, Chan shot the judge a disgruntled look. His expression changed little as he read. Jaw clenching, he refolded the paper, handing it back to Collins. "You've been busy."

"Better to get disagreeable items out of the way early, don't you think?"

"What I think, Judge, is it's a dirty trick."

"I'll do whatever is needed to keep a valuable man under my employ. Ulysses agrees with me."

"Ulysses?" Beth asked, warning bells ringing in her head.

"I felt it urgent enough to send off an emergency telegram to the president. He sleeps little, so I figured he'd respond quickly."

Even Thad was surprised. "You know the president?"

Collins chuckled at the expressions on the three faces. "We were boys together in Georgetown, Ohio. He hated his father's tannery, and I had no intention of following my father as a shopkeeper. Ulysses received an appointment to West Point, and I went on to college in northern New York. We've kept in touch over the years." He set the telegram on the table, stabbing it with a finger. "He agreed this investigation is important. Stopping counterfeiters is crucial to keeping the citizens' faith in our currency. The president wants the best people possible working the assignment, and you three are the best."

Chan let out a frustrated breath. "I know *nothing* about stopping coney men, Judge."

Ignoring him, Collins slid the telegram into a pocket and stood. "You're a fast learner with incredible instincts. These two," he nodded at Thad and Beth, "are the best teachers you could get. Take advantage of their knowledge, use your own experience, and help us locate and arrest the people responsible for passing those bogus bills. I have a full schedule today, so I'll leave you three to work out the details."

Chan felt squeezed, as if in a vise, unable to move or break free. The president had ordered him to accept the assignment. As a U.S. Marshal, Grant was his ultimate commander, a man who knew how to exert pressure.

Picking up his badge, he pinned it to his shirt and leaned forward. He met their expectant gazes, cold eyes sparking with disgust.

"Look, Chan—"

He cut Beth off with a wave of his hand. "I see nothing's changed. You'll use any means necessary to get what you want. Now that you've manipulated the truth to get me to work with you, tell me what you have. I'll do what I can, but I work alone."

"That doesn't work for us."

"It doesn't matter, Agent Taylor. Neither Collins nor Grant said we had to work as a team, unless you want to run to the judge again and lodge a formal complaint." A slight amount of satisfaction warmed Chan when Thad shifted in his chair. "Tell me what you have, we divide up the duties, and I'll be on my way."

Beth squared her shoulders, tired of his unconcealed arrogance. "We handle investigations as a team, Chan."

"Not true, Mrs. Cartman. We certainly weren't a team back in Austin." Somewhat of a lie, as they had found a way to work together. "You were a solo agent back then. If the two of you want to travel together, duplicate each interview, then do it. Me? I work alone. Unless you want to waste more time, I suggest you explain what you have."

Silence fell over the table, the two agents considering the latest snag. A minute passed before Thad stood, motioning for the others to do the same.

"Let's talk at the jail where we can't be overheard."

It took little time to traverse the short distance between the hotel and jail. Sterling sat behind his desk, shuffling through wanted posters. The sheriff didn't offer to leave so they could have privacy, and Thad didn't ask.

Sterling reached into a drawer, sliding a leather folio toward Thad. Unfolding it, the agent pulled out a sheath of papers, handing them to Chan.

"This is what we have so far. You'll see why the leads pointed to Big Pine and Splendor. They may be false, but we have to follow them until we know for certain."

Chan read each page, taking his time, mentally cataloging his questions. There wasn't much. Several interviews in Austin and Kansas City. "The postmaster was the one who told you the packages came from Splendor?"

"Yes. None of the recipients were around to interview. They'd disappeared, as if knowing someone would be coming to Kansas City," Thad said.

Chan looked at Beth, lifting a brow. "You weren't with him?"

"No. I traveled to Austin while Thad went to Kansas City. As my notes show, there was one good lead. Mort Miller owned a ranch not far out of town. When I interviewed him, he spotted a couple men at another table. Something about them spooked Miller and he took off. Captain Jones rode with me to his ranch, but by the time we got there, a few days had passed and he was gone."

"Your notes say he packed up everything and left the ranch behind," Chan said.

"The bank would've taken it back anyway. Miller hadn't made a payment in several months. Guess he figured the time had come to leave his troubles behind."

"Including the men who'd spooked him."

Beth gave a slow nod. "I believe so."

"There are no sender names in your notes for the packages from Splendor."

"Names weren't shown. Only the town," Thad said.

"Anything distinctive about the writing?" Chan asked.

"Nothing."

Chan turned toward Beth. "Were you able to find out if there were packages from Splendor sent to Mort Miller in Austin?"

"Unfortunately, no. I wanted to talk to him about the men who spooked him. There was definitely a connection between them, and I'm certain it has to do with fake notes."

"Why?"

Frustration ebbed through her before she hid her reaction. She grasped the edges of the chair, voice tight. "He took bogus funds into one of the Austin banks. The manager spotted them as fakes and took them to the sheriff. He sent a couple to us, which triggered my trip.”

Other than a brief nod, Chan showed no reaction. “So we forget about Miller for now.”

“Agreed. How do we locate whoever sent the packages from Splendor?” Beth asked.

Setting the documents on Sterling’s desk, Chan leaned back. “You understand the packages could’ve been mailed from anywhere. Because they showed Splendor doesn’t mean that’s where they were posted.”

Beth cast a glance at Thad. They’d discussed it, dismissing the idea as being potentially too complicated. Not for them, but for the coney men. She now doubted the wisdom of their decision.

As if reading her mind, Chan stretched out his legs, crossing them at the ankles. He held up one of the fake notes.

“Anyone who takes the amount of time needed to create this intricate artwork and plates is talented and shrewd. My guess is this was a tactic to throw off agents such as yourself. They could’ve been sent from Deadwood, Dodge City, or Denver. It doesn’t mean I won’t look in Splendor, but you two should consider there are other possibilities.”

Thad picked up the stack of papers, scanning them for what he wanted. “There were two potential leads in Omaha and another in St. Louis. Possibles exist in Nashville and Springfield, Illinois. The problem is we don’t have enough agents to follow them.”

Chan thought the solution easy. "I'll take care of the Montana Territory. You and Beth head back to Omaha and work the leads from there."

Thad stared at him, jaw clenched, lips drawn into a thin line. Picking up the papers, he set a few aside, sliding the rest back into the folio and standing.

"I agree with much of what you've said, Marshal. Based on that, I'll tell you how we're going to proceed."

Nostrils flaring, the muscles in Chan's jaw worked. "Go on."

"I've left you the information we have for the Montana Territory."

Shoving up, Chan grabbed them. Folding the papers, he slipped them into a pocket. "Good. I'll be on my way."

"Not alone."

Back stiffening, Chan's gaze narrowed, his chocolate brown eyes changing to a deep umber. "What do you mean?"

"I can take care of the leads outside of this area. You, though, need an experienced agent by your side. That's why Agent Cartman is sticking to you, Marshal. She's your new partner."

Chapter Twelve

Chan stormed from the jail after arguing with Thad over the pros and cons of Beth staying with him. The heated discussion centered on Chan's lack of knowledge about tracking counterfeiters, a point the senior agent had to concede. It still didn't sway his order for Beth to partner with the marshal.

Thad would be taking the stage east, leaving Beth behind. If Chan didn't like it, he was free to speak with Judge Collins.

There'd been no real choice. Thad knew Chan wouldn't take his grievance to the judge, refusing to voice his displeasure about partnering with Beth.

"Chan. Wait."

Stopping, he turned to face her with a somber expression. "Do you have a horse?"

Beth halted a few feet away. Squaring her shoulders, she lifted her chin, jutting it toward him. "No, but I'll have one by morning."

"I'm going to the livery and will select a horse for you."

"You will *not*. I'll pick out my own horse." She attempted to walk past him, stopping when he snagged her arm.

"The horses out here aren't docile. They take a firm hand, and—"

"Don't patronize me." Tearing away from his grasp, she crossed her arms. "I've been riding my entire life, and as you'll recall, I am quite accomplished. You are welcome to come with me to the livery, but *I* will select my own horse." Daring him to stop her again, she walked past.

Resting his hands on his hips, Chan shook his head, but followed. She'd need a saddle and tack, as well as saddlebags. If they were going to ride together, he'd make certain she was ready for the long ride to Splendor.

Catching up to her, Chan kept pace on their way to the livery. "Splendor is a small town. The last I heard, it's about half the size of Big Pine. It won't take more than one person to search for any link to the counterfeiters. Your skills would be better utilized by going with Thad."

She said nothing.

"There are several deputies, including ex-Texas Rangers and ex-Pinkerton agents, who will volunteer to help."

Beth didn't spare him a glance. Entering the blacksmith shop, she spotted a man of average height with thick, muscled arms and hands the size of ham bones. Noticing their presence, he straightened, setting down the hammer.

"What do you need?"

"I'm looking for a horse."

The blacksmith looked past her to Chan. "Marshal. She with you?"

Irritation had her stalking closer to him. "I'm the one purchasing the horse. You'll be dealing with me."

His mouth tilted into a grin, the rebuke not bothering him at all. "Yes, ma'am." Walking through the gate to the livery, he pointed to the stalls. "Those four are what I have. One mare and three geldings."

"Do you own them?"

"Sure do. I can answer your questions, too," he smirked.

Beth walked straight to the first stall, asked a few questions then moved to the next, until she'd studied each of the horses.

"What do you want for the gelding in the third stall?"

He named a price, which she accepted.

"I'll need a saddle, tack, and saddlebags."

"It'd be best to try the saddlery across the street. He'll have what you need. When do you plan to take the horse?"

She looked at Chan, lifting a brow.

"First light tomorrow," he answered.

"Bring me your saddle and tack, and I'll have the horse ready, ma'am."

"What about Caesar?"

"You can tack your own horse, Marshal."

Lightning shot through the sky, one bolt after another, as rain pounded the ground. It had been this way for hours, since not long after midnight.

Chan leaned against the wall, peering out the window of his hotel room at the drenched ground. An hour before dawn and he already knew the trail to Splendor would be too treacherous to travel until the rain let up and another day passed, allowing the thick, sticky mud to dry. At least enough so the horses' legs wouldn't be sucked to well above their cannons.

Cursing, he turned away from the window. Staying in Big Pine at least two more days held no appeal, not after spotting the gunman in Splendor, a man Chan knew wanted him dead. And definitely not with Beth in a room on the same floor. Thad would be leaving on the afternoon stage, transportation undeterred by most weather conditions. Although the soggy ground might be too much for even the four-wheeled coach.

A soft knock had him opening the door. Beth stood in the hall, dark circles under her eyes.

"The storm keep you awake, too?" He stepped aside for her to pass.

"Yes." She walked straight to the window and looked out. "Will we be leaving today?"

He joined her, stopping a couple feet away. "No, and not tomorrow, either. We need the ground dry enough so the horses don't break a leg."

She touched the pendant hanging from a chain around her neck. He'd seen her do it many times when thinking. If he remembered right, it was a gift from her late husband. Something she never removed.

"Two more days," she whispered.

"Assuming the weather lets up today. If not, it could be longer."

Shifting, she studied him, as if making a decision. "We're going to be spending time together, Chan. I know the last time—"

He held up a hand, interrupting her. "What happened between us was a mistake."

She sucked in a breath, a lance of pain spearing through her. "I never thought it a mistake."

A brow lifted. "That's why you disappeared in the middle of the night after leaving a terse note?"

"I…"

He turned away, shaking his head. "A mistake, Beth. Nothing more."

She didn't agree, but now wasn't the time to argue. "Do you think we could at least call a truce during the investigation?"

Stopping, he glanced over his shoulder. "Sure. If there's nothing else, I'm heading downstairs for breakfast." Chan opened the door, indicating she should leave.

Walking past him, she stopped long enough to give him an appraising look. "I intend to solve this case, with or without your help."

Closing the door, he followed her along the hall. "You'll have my help, Agent Cartman. Just remember that you and Thad got me into this."

They didn't spend the next two days sitting around, waiting for the weather to clear and trail to dry. No proof existed pointing to anyone in Big Pine receiving packages, but interviewing local businesses could be productive and fill their time.

Dividing up the town, they entered shops, hotels, restaurants, and banks, talking to the owners and patrons rather than conducting interviews. Instead of learning little, they came up with too much information. Seemed a lot of people in the territorial capital had friends or relatives in Splendor. Letters and packages flowed between the two towns often enough to be meaningless.

"Will the trail be dry enough to leave for Splendor tomorrow?" Beth sliced a piece of steak. She'd met Chan in the dining room of their hotel for supper.

He'd been nothing more than cordial and professional. Far different from the attentive lover of two years before.

"If another storm doesn't come through tonight, we leave at dawn." Chan finished the last bite of his meal, draining his cup of coffee. Standing, he tossed coins on the table. "I'll see you tomorrow."

"Where are you going?" She winced as soon as the question left her lips.

He stilled for a moment, studying her. "To the saloon."

Beth watched him leave, following his path along the boardwalk until he disappeared. A slow ache grew in her chest, the remainder of her food forgotten. Nodding when the server offered more coffee, she pushed her plate away. She found herself thinking of their weeks together in Austin, how close they'd become, and how she'd thrown it all away.

Enough time had passed since Abner's death for her to understand how much she'd lost by leaving Chan. She recalled the series of events leading to her departure.

With the bank robbers on their way to trial in New York, Thad had ordered her home for a new assignment. She'd replied, asking if there might be a case which could be worked from Austin. His response had been one word.

No.

Beth had a choice to make. Stay and lose her job, or leave and lose Chan. Coupled with her doubts about falling in love so soon after her husband's death, and Chan's age, the decision hadn't been hard. Not then anyway.

Although him being a few years younger still nagged at her, she no longer had doubts about her feelings. She loved him then and loved him more now.

Holding the cup with both hands, she stared into it. The time had come to accept Chan no longer held any interest in her, would never forgive her hasty retreat. Worse, Beth knew she'd feel the same if their situations were reversed. In fact, she might not be as civil to him as he'd been to her. Distant, cold, and professional.

Beth would do what had always saved her in the past. Concentrate on the assignment, hunt down and arrest the crooks, then move on to the next job.

Not ready to return to her room, she finished the coffee and walked outside. It was a clear night with a slight breeze and no sign of rain.

Sucking in a comforting breath, she headed straight to the livery. She'd stopped by each of the last two days to visit her sorrel gelding, Buckshot. Beth had yet to ride him and couldn't wait for the trip in the morning. He had a good disposition, wonderful lines, and from what the blacksmith had told her, a lot of spirit.

Opening the gate, she stopped outside his stall. "Hello, Buckshot."

At the sound of her voice, the gelding whinnied and walked toward her. Raising his head over the top rail, she stroked his nose, the same as she'd done with each visit. The feel of him soothed Beth in a way she couldn't explain.

She'd grown up with horses, learning to ride at a young age. After accepting a position as a government agent, Beth found herself using buggies, trains, and stagecoaches for most travel. The exceptions occurred when the job landed her in places such as Austin, as had happened two years earlier.

Chan told her it would be several hours to Splendor over mostly flat terrain. The trip didn't appear to be a problem until he mentioned the renegade band of Crow who patrolled the trail, watching for an opportunity to steal weapons or provisions.

She and Chan had come across Apaches in northern Texas and Oklahoma while tracking the bank robbers. Their presence had been more threatening than real. After learning the Crow had been the ones to shoot Chan, Beth realized the depth of the danger.

Regardless of the peril, she felt a jolt of excitement at leaving Big Pine and resuming the investigation. All her instincts screamed Splendor would hold the answers to identify the counterfeiters, as well as other questions burning in her gut.

Chapter Thirteen

Cheyenne, Wyoming Territory

Gyp Slade leveled his gun and pulled the trigger, chuckling in satisfaction when the empty can flew off the tree stump. Holstering the six-shooter, he readied himself for the three remaining cans. Arms slack at his sides, feet planted shoulder width apart, he expelled a breath, drew, and fired three shots in quick succession.

"Two out of three isn't bad, Gyp." Hugh Fisher stood a few feet away, his brother, Harvey, next to him.

"I nicked it. I'm sure of it," Gyp growled.

"If you'd nicked it, the can would be on the ground," Harvey muttered, more than ready for his turn.

Gyp shifted toward him. "What's that, Fisher?"

"Nothing. You done?"

Motioning with his gun, Gyp shoved it into the holster, stepping aside. Harvey had already placed three cans on a nearby boulder, not far from where Hugh's cans waited on another, flatter rock.

Harvey stared at the targets, flexing his fingers, letting the air flow from his lungs. Less than five seconds later, six cans lay on the ground. His and Hugh's.

"Damn. That's some good shooting." His brother didn't comment on his three cans being blown apart. "You've been practicing."

Harvey didn't answer, his wary gaze focused on Gyp. You never knew what he'd do in any situation, which had begun to disturb Harvey more with each passing week.

He and Hugh had been riding with Gyp for a while. All had gone well for a time, the money working for Simon Priest beyond their imaginings. They'd hoarded away almost enough to buy the ranch they'd talked about since they were boys. Then things started to change.

The future they'd dreamed of began to fade the longer they rode with Gyp, the brothers growing more cautious of his changing moods. One minute he was congenial. Ready to blow someone's head off the next.

They knew Gyp had received a letter from Priest the day before, explaining their next job. This one involved robbing the stage from Big Pine to Moosejaw. Priest had been specific about what they were to take, and as always, adamant the passengers were to remain unharmed.

The payoff to them would be similar to their previous jobs. For Hugh and Harvey, this meant they'd have enough to leave Gyp behind and buy their ranch. Staying longer would provide more funds, but neither was comfortable with a partner who might turn on them at any time for no reason.

"When do we leave for the job?" Hugh's question was meant to ease the tension between Harvey and Gyp, which hadn't lessened since his brother shot the six cans.

Tearing his gaze from Harvey, Gyp walked to his horse, then spun back around. A bullet hit the ground less than a foot from Harvey's feet.

"What the hell?"

"Just reminding you who's boss around here, Harvey."

"Never said you weren't, Gyp."

"It's what you're thinking."

Hugh stepped between them, hands held out to his sides. "Put the gun away, Gyp. We've got a job coming up, and you can't afford to lose either of us."

"You and I can handle the job, Hugh." He continued pointing the gun at Harvey.

"Can't be done. Three is the minimum needed to stop and rob a stage. One with a gun on the driver, one on the guard, and the third on the passengers. Now, settle down and let's ride back to town for supper."

No one spoke for several minutes, the tension growing until Gyp threw his head back and laughed. "Ah, hell. You boys are too damn serious." Shoving the gun into its holster, he mounted. "Let's go."

Neither brother moved. Jaw clenched, Harvey kept his hand on the butt of his gun.

"Are you two coming?"

Hugh and Harvey exchanged hard-edged looks. It would be smart to get as far away from Gyp as possible, but not now. They'd wait until he'd gotten falling-down drunk, then make their move, forgetting about the job in the Montana Territory and Gyp Slade.

Chan rode ahead of Beth, his attention focused on the surrounding hills, his thoughts on the woman behind him. They'd been on the trail for two hours with no sign of the Crow or the occasional bandit who'd been known to raid stagecoaches and those on horseback.

He'd thought through what needed to be done once they reached Splendor. His first stop would be the telegraph and post office. Bernie Griggs was the only clerk in the history of the town, and scrupulous in his duty. If anyone noticed suspicious behavior, it would be Bernie.

Whatever leads he provided could be split between Chan and Beth. If the forgers were working out of Splendor, they'd shut them down, and Agent Cartman would be on her way. A prospect which both eased his mind and deepened the hole in his heart.

They'd spoken little since leaving Big Pine, which suited Chan fine. When working together before, there'd been a comfortable silence, neither feeling the need to fill the quiet with empty words.

Today was different, the tension between them thick. Hence the reason they rode so far apart. At least six feet separated them, too much distance in the hostile land they had to traverse.

Slowing Caesar so Beth could catch up, Chan said nothing, letting the silence continue. He saw no need to talk unless about the investigation, and that topic could wait until arriving in Splendor.

Caesar's slight whinny had him whipping his head one direction, then another, gaze coming to a stop on a hill a few hundred yards away. Five horses with riders in a single line stared in their direction. The band of renegade Crow.

"What should we do, Chan?"

Tearing his attention away from the riders, he spared her a short glance. "Nothing yet."

"Nothing?"

"We keep watch. If they make a move to ride closer, you do exactly as I say."

"But—"

"But nothing, Beth. This is my territory and you'll follow my orders." He ignored the way she bristled. "We'll move a little farther south, away from the hill. If the threat becomes real, there's another trail into Splendor. Stay right with me." Glancing at her again, his lips twitched at her resolute gaze and pinched lips. She might not like taking orders from him, but Beth wasn't a fool. The case wouldn't go any further if they were dead.

With each step, their horses drew farther away from the five Crow, who hadn't moved since first being spotted. Chan found their behavior curious. A week ago, they'd chased and wounded him. Today, they sat motionless.

Noticing Beth had dropped too far behind, he motioned her forward without losing focus on the Crow.

They were almost at the point where they'd need to either continue on the main trail to Splendor or rein south to the alternate route. The original trail would get them there sooner, but they'd be more exposed. The southern course would take longer while providing better cover.

"Do they appear to be moving to you?" Beth asked.

"Not toward us. They're riding along the crest of the hill. It doesn't mean they won't change their minds and attack." He leaned back, resting his hand on the scabbard holding his rifle.

Both he and Beth had six-shooters, a rifle, and a shotgun. If attacked, they'd be able to do some serious damage.

"Are they the ones who shot you?" She nodded toward his arm.

"I never got a good look. Too busy trying to stay alive. I am certain they were from the same renegade group."

"How much longer will they track us?"

"There's no way to know, Beth. It may not be us they want."

"What do you mean?"

Chan had considered the stagecoach between Splendor and Big Pine for a while. The Crow usually attacked one or two riders, but they'd been known to raid stages and wagons, killing to get what they wanted and taking captives, as they'd done with Dom's wife, Josie. He pulled out his pocket watch.

"The stage from Splendor is due any time."

"We can't leave them to fend off the Crow."

He heard the slight tremble in Beth's voice, as well as an underlying resolve. She wouldn't ride off if there remained a chance innocent people could be hurt. It was part of why he loved her. Or *had* loved her.

"No, we can't, but I refuse to put you in danger." When he saw her face harden, his hand tightened on the reins, readying himself.

"It's not your decision, Chan. I wear a badge the same as you."

"Not quite the same, Beth."

"We're both federal employees and ultimately report to the president. I can shoot as well as you."

"While atop your horse? How do you know Buckshot won't spook and buck you off?"

"I can handle him." Leaning forward, she stroked the gelding's neck, sending Chan a smug grin. "You'll just have to get used to it. If you guard the stagecoach, so do I."

"Beth…" Chan saw the look in her eyes and stopped. She'd made her decision, and he knew there'd be no changing it.

"Should we ride closer to the main trail?"

"Not yet. We'll wait until we see the stage over the horizon. If the Crow make a move, so do we."

Shouts and gunfire erupted seconds after Chan spoke. The stage came into view, the guard turning to aim at the riders approaching from the crest of the hill.

Pulling his rifle from its scabbard, Chan kicked Caesar. He didn't spare Beth a glance, knowing she'd be right behind him. Wrapping the reins once around the saddlehorn, he guided his horse with his thighs and knees while lifting the rifle. He aimed and fired twice, toppling one of the riders from his horse.

Behind him, another shot rang out. Beth missed, made a correction, and shot again, hitting her target. Taking a quick glance over his shoulder, his chest squeezed at the image she made.

She guided Buckshot the same as Chan, legs gripping the gelding's sides, arms free to aim and fire. Approaching the stage, both settled the butt of their rifles, lowering them when the last two Crow rode off. They'd each hit one, the guard another.

The driver reined up, the guard jumping down to check the passengers. Chan and Beth rode to the other side of the stagecoach, taking positions so they could watch the renegades disappear over the hill.

"Thanks for your help, Marshal."

"Glad we were in the area, Ervin." Chan liked the young driver with an easy smile and gregarious manner. "We can escort you on to Big Pine."

"No need, Marshal. I've never known the Crow to return after riding off. It may be time to request help from Fort Connall."

"I doubt it will help. I've met the commander a couple times, and he's not too interested in helping civilians."

Scratching the stubble on his chin, his eyes twinkled. "Guess it's up to the rest of us. We'd best get going. Be careful, Marshal." Ervin shot a look at Beth, his meaning clear.

"We plan to be."

The stage took off, a couple young passengers waving to him and Beth, fear still showing on their faces.

"Time for us to head out." He studied her face, seeing beads of sweat on her forehead, eyes pinched with worry or fear...or both.

Chapter Fourteen

Splendor

Francesca O'Reilly hung her law degree on a nail, standing back, cocking a brow before adjusting it enough to make it level. She'd been in town a short time and already had several clients, including the Pelletier brothers. Noah Brandt and his wife, Abby, would be coming in that afternoon.

The long trip from New York had been a gamble. She'd worked hard to build her practice and prove herself. It had been a battle, every client hard-won. Even her family had never moved their legal work to her. Their lack of action had been a blow to her pride, ultimately leading to her decision to leave.

After many evenings talking with friends of hers and Rachel's, five had committed to the move. Two were teachers, two nurses, and herself.

Francesca had taken over the law office left behind by a previous attorney who'd been killed by bank robbers. Another lawyer had come to town for a short while, but left after making the decision to move back to Boston. This forced the residents to move their legal matters to attorneys in Big Pine.

The Bank of Splendor's president, Horace Clausen, had offered her excellent terms to take over the office space, volunteering to pass on word about her arrival.

Her friendship with Rachel helped the most in gaining clients. She couldn't be more pleased with her decision to leave New York.

"Miss O'Reilly?"

Turning, a smile crossed her face. "Deputy Boudreaux. What a nice surprise. Please, have a seat."

"I can't stay long. Just wanted to make sure you were getting settled." Zeke Boudreaux held his hat in both hands, his fingers worrying the edges of the brim.

She waved her hand through the air. "As you can see, there's still a lot to get done, but I'm making progress."

Zeke's gaze moved over her, taking in the silky auburn hair, bright green eyes, and the way she filled out the simple dress. She'd been a sight when they'd first met at the Pelletier ranch, drawing him to her as a fly to honey. Today was no different.

Tongue thick, throat dry, Zeke looked down at his hat. "Yes, ma'am, you are."

Taking a couple steps closer, Francesca studied his face. "Are you feeling all right, Deputy? You look a little peaked."

Jerking his head up, he met her gaze. "I'm fine, Miss O'Reilly. Well, guess I'd better get going. Let me know if there's anything you need."

Crossing her arms, Francesca watched him close the door, wondering what just happened. They'd talked for a long time at the reception Rachel gave for her five friends, then danced two or three times.

Between Zeke, his brother, Hex, Chan Evans, and all the Pelletier friends, she'd had a wonderful time. And the attention was a big boost to her self-esteem.

There'd been another reason for leaving New York, one few people knew about. Francesca wasn't a stupid woman, except one time in a moment of passion. She'd succumbed to her fiancé's pressure to make love. Between that night and two months later, he'd ended the betrothal, leaving her alone and pregnant.

Francesca had wanted the baby, but it wasn't to be. She'd lost it in her third month during a painful, gut-wrenching night. Not one person ever knew of her condition, especially her family. She'd taken a long time to recover. Rachel's invitation to move west had come at the perfect time.

A soft knock preceded Rachel entering the office. "I hoped you'd be in here. Oh, you've gotten so much done, Frannie."

Francesca grinned at the nickname. Few people ever called her by it, Rachel being one. "It's taken a few days, but I'm almost finished."

"I came to take you to lunch, assuming you have time."

Placing a hand on her stomach, Francesca had a brief thought of the baby she'd lost. Shaking the unwelcome memory aside, she picked up her reticule.

"I'd love to get away from this for a while."

"Good, because I have more clients for you, and they'll be at the Eagle's Nest." Rachel turned around, leaving the office before Francesca could respond.

Chan and Beth rode into Splendor late in the afternoon, hungry, tired, and ready for baths. Lifting his hand to return several greetings, he led her straight to the jail, hoping his brother would be inside.

Dismounting, he resisted the urge to help Beth to the ground. Like in Austin, she'd proven herself in a difficult situation, coming out shaken, but otherwise unhurt. He had to keep reminding himself she was a trained federal agent who hunted criminals for a living, not an East Coast debutante. A woman with brains, beauty, and a deep devotion to justice. The woman he wanted, but could never have.

Shoving the door open, he motioned for her to enter before him, relieved to see Gabe at his desk. The sheriff stood at Beth's entry.

"You must be Chan's brother, Gabriel."

"And you are?"

"Federal Agent Elizabeth Cartman." She held out her hand, an unusual gesture for a woman.

Gabe glanced at it a moment before engulfing her hand in his much larger one. "Agent Cartman. It's a pleasure." Releasing his grip, he motioned for her to take a seat. "What brings you to Splendor?"

"Counterfeiters, Sheriff."

Brows lifting, he sat down, resting his arms on the desk. "You believe you'll find them here?"

"The leads we have indicate it's possible. We've recruited Marshal Evans to help us."

"That so, Chan?"

Grabbing a chair, he lowered himself into it. "Afraid it is. They've got some evidence indicating forged bank notes may be originating right here."

"They?" Gabe asked.

"Thaddeus Taylor, the senior agent on this investigation, and his superiors," Beth said.

"What makes you believe the notes come from here?"

The door opened, stalling any response. Two of Gabe's deputies, Cash Coulter and Beau Davis, walked in, removing their hats when they spotted Beth.

"Ma'am," Cash and Beau said in unison.

"Deputies. I'm Elizabeth Cartman."

"She's a federal agent trying to solve a counterfeiting case," Gabe said. "Chan is working with her. There's evidence the notes may be printed here."

"In Splendor?" Beau's voice held a hint of incredulity.

"Possibly," Chan answered. "Packages containing fake bills showed up in Kansas City, all with Splendor as the return address."

"Anything else?" Cash asked.

"Only the town. My partner tried to find the people who received them, but they'd left town. The one person I was able to interview in Austin got spooked," Beth said, disgusted. "He packed up and left his ranch behind. No idea where he and his wife went."

"What spooked him?" Beau asked.

"We were in a restaurant when two men walked in, taking a table not far from ours. The rancher, Mort Miller, got nervous and left. By the time I followed, he'd disappeared."

Gabe rubbed the back of his neck, considering what Beth had told them. "Your only connection to Splendor is the address on a package?"

"According to the Kansas City postmaster, more than one."

Gabe met Chan's gaze before returning his attention to Beth. "Anyone could've put whatever town they wanted on the package."

"Chan already mentioned that, Sheriff."

"Then you already know Splendor could've been written to draw you off the counterfeiter's trail."

"Yes, but not following the clues is unthinkable. If there's no credibility to them, we'll start over." She glanced at Chan, seeing him narrow his gaze on her. "Thad and I will start over."

Her words should've comforted him, but they didn't. Chan realized he wanted the forgers to be in Splendor, wanted more time with Beth.

"First, we must determine if the address means anything," he said.

"How can we help?" Gabe asked.

Cullen Burris leaned against a post down the boardwalk. The decision he'd made to stay in Splendor had been a good one. He'd spent the time learning all he could about the Evans brothers, where they lived, and family members. Everything any gunfighter could use to get to the person targeted.

He'd been having a drink in the Dixie when Chan Evans rode back into town with a woman Burris didn't recognize. They'd entered the jail, been in there quite a while before leaving. Their next stop had been the St. James Hotel, where he assumed the woman had taken a room.

Shortly afterward, Evans had left the hotel. Burris watched as he made a brief stop in the Dixie, then moved on to the telegraph office. His visit there hadn't lasted long. Instead of riding out of town to the Lucero ranch, Evans had taken the trail to his brother's home. He hadn't followed.

Figuring the marshal would settle in at the sheriff's for the night, Burris had taken a table in the restaurant owned by Suzanne Barnett. The food was good and plentiful.

The restaurant was where he did his thinking, planned how he'd kill the marshal in the slowest way possible without getting caught. Evans's demise would be his path to freedom.

Killing the only witness to a murder assured Burris could never be convicted of that murder. At least not the one Evans stumbled upon in Austin. A deputy had tried to take the gunslinger into custody for killing a Texas Ranger and bank manager. He'd been foolish to try and take a trained gunfighter to jail by himself. It had been stupid for Burris's younger brother to go along with him. An accountant with limited experience brandishing a weapon, he'd been an innocent.

Evans had been after him for the killing of a fellow Ranger. He'd come upon Burris and the deputy the moment the outlaw had pointed a gun at the young man and fired. Shifting, he'd fired on Evans. The Texas Ranger had returned fire, killing Burris's brother. He hadn't stayed around to mourn. Instead, he'd plotted his revenge.

It had taken the outlaw a long time to find Evans, surprised he'd ended up in a small frontier town in Montana. Burris could almost taste the thrill of retribution. After all this time, he'd soon be able to avenge his brother and go on with his own life.

Chapter Fifteen

Kansas City

Damien Priest tossed back another shot of whiskey, rubbing the stump of his missing leg. He preferred liquid pain killer to becoming addicted to the laudanum his doctor had prescribed. Priest had seen too many Confederate soldiers succumb to the drug, needing increasing amounts to dull the constant throbbing from the loss of a limb or other injury during battle.

Voices from the entry broke the peace of a solitary evening. His circle of friends was small, and few of those ever came by for a visit. He didn't know who else it could be, knowing it wouldn't take long to find out.

The door shoved open, his younger brother, Simon, entering. "Good evening, Damien." He held up his hand when his brother began to rise. "Don't get up."

Picking up the empty shot glass on the desk, he refilled it with whiskey, as well as poured some for himself. Handing the one back to Damien, he sat across the desk.

"I thought it was time we talked about distribution."

"Your timing is perfect, Simon. I've been working on a revised plan most of the day. This saves me a trip to Omaha."

Simon threw back his head and laughed. "When was the last time you traveled to my home?"

Damien's features sobered. "I don't recall ever being there."

"Because you haven't. Do you want to go over your ideas tonight or wait until morning?"

"Tonight, unless you're too tired from the trip."

"Let's do it now," Simon said.

Shoving a neatly penned paper across the table, Damien began running a finger down the page. "Our decision to split the printing between Denver and Splendor has proved to be excellent. I'm considering adding two more locations."

Simon's brows shot up, but he said nothing. His brother was a brilliant businessman, the same as he'd been an excellent Confederate officer. If he hadn't lost his leg in the war, Damien would be a leader in the reconstruction of the South.

Instead, he became a major force in amassing the money desperately required for a second fight for secession. His efforts now focused on expanding the counterfeiting operations, saving the money in several banks in states still friendly to the Confederate cause. At the rate their savings were rising, they'd have enough in five years to execute an attack on Washington.

During this time, an elite group of southern gentlemen were recruiting and training men. They were part of a highly secretive cadre of ex-Confederate officers, businessmen, and a few landowners who'd been able to salvage their properties.

"Milwaukee and Nashville."

"Why those?" Simon read Damien's notes under each city. Population, transportation, contacts already in place.

"They're larger than Denver and much bigger than Splendor. Adding these two will give us bases in four diverse locations with different layers of distribution. If one is discovered, the other three will continue to operate."

"Are there sufficient layers to protect our identities?" Simon sat back, crossing his arms.

"Of course."

"Four locations increase the risk to us, Damien. It will take more than me to monitor two additional cities."

"You will continue with Denver and Splendor, adding either Milwaukee or Nashville. Your choice. I'll take care of whichever city is left."

"Your leg won't allow you to travel that much, Damien."

"You mean my *lack* of a leg. I appreciate your concern, but traveling won't be a problem."

Simon considered his brother's injury, the way it agonized him more in cold weather. "I'll handle distribution out of Milwaukee. Nashville is closer to Kansas City and an easy trip for you by train. Have you already made contact with the post office of each city?"

"Not personally. Those identified have been offered four times what they're making now to act as our intermediary."

"We need to make a decision on Splendor."

Damien shoved back in his chair, stretching out his good leg, rubbing the stump of the other.

Grabbing his brother's glass, Simon filled it with whiskey, handing it over. "Drink this, then I'll pour another."

Simon knew of Damien's preference to numb his pain with alcohol rather than laudanum. He drank only enough to ease the ache, not dull his senses, which meant constant small amounts of whiskey.

Tossing it back, Damien set the glass down. "Of the four locations, Splendor's postmaster is the only one we were unable to approach. He works alone, and as you've been told, takes great pride in his position."

"*Incorruptible* is what I learned. I should've done a better job when suggesting Splendor."

"It's done, Simon. We either move the equipment out of Splendor or continue shipments, as we're doing now."

"No one suspects us of using such a remote location. After we have Milwaukee and Nashville in operation, we can make a change."

Damien narrowed his gaze. "Are you certain no one suspects Splendor?"

"We've been careful. Our contact there says he's heard of no one asking about fake notes."

"Can the contact still be trusted?"

Simon chuckled. "For what we pay, yes."

"You need to ride there and make certain."

Dragging a hand down his face, Simon nodded. "I'll leave for Milwaukee in the morning. Once I'm finished there, I'll ride through Denver to Cheyenne, but I can't show my face in Montana."

"Let me know your progress in Milwaukee. If you don't like what you see, we'll choose another city."

Simon studied his brother's face a moment before giving him a sharp nod. "I will."

Splendor

Chan's eyes cracked open, shifting to look out the window. Still dark. The night hadn't been a good one. He'd gone to bed after a brief conversation with Gabe over supper. Lena, their son, Jack, and Walter Evans had listened, not commenting as he explained a little about his involvement in the counterfeiting investigation.

Jack had thought it wonderful to have his uncle working with a federal agent. Lena and Walter were more interested in the fact President Grant ordered him to work on the case.

Afterward, he had a couple glasses of whiskey with Gabe before going to bed. Sleep never came. His mind moved between the investigation, Beth's presence, and Cullen Burris. He hadn't seen the outlaw after arriving in Splendor, although that meant nothing.

Rolling out of bed, he dressed and headed downstairs. Except for faint moonlight streaming through the windows, the house was dark. Threading fingers through his hair, he made his way to the kitchen.

By the location of the moon, he figured it would be another two hours before the first morning rays came over the eastern hills. Knowing none of the restaurants would be open, he made coffee, cut a thick slice of bread, and slathered it with the jam Lena had put up that summer.

"Thought I heard you moving around down here." Gabe grabbed two cups, poured coffee into each, handing one to Chan.

"Couldn't sleep."

"Understandable. You were attacked by the Crow, shot, ordered to take on work you don't want, and foiled a raid on the stagecoach. Plus, you're saddled with a woman you don't know."

Sitting and stretching out his legs, Chan sipped his coffee, deciding it was time to share his history with Beth. "We worked together one other time."

"When?"

He explained how they'd hunted a group of bank robbers who'd stolen from a federal bank.

"It took a few weeks." Chan cleared his throat and took another swallow of coffee, drumming his fingers on the table. "We became close."

Gabe's eyes widened in surprise. "How close?"

Sucking in a breath, Chan let it out in a slow whoosh. "Very close. I fell in love with her, Gabe." He waited several beats before continuing. "I believed she felt the same."

His brother listened, features showing nothing of what he thought.

"One morning she was gone, leaving a short note, nothing more. I hadn't seen or heard from her until she showed up in Big Pine with her partner."

"Thaddeus Taylor."

Chan nodded. "Right."

"Do you still feel the same about her?"

"Hell no. She made her choice. I certainly didn't wait around for her to return."

Gabe looked skeptical.

"Beth was still in love with her dead husband, as well as her job back east. It never would've worked out between us. It was for the best."

Instead of responding, Gabe stood, refilled their cups, and leaned against the counter. "Enoch told me about the gunfighter you recognized before leaving for Big Pine. You should've told me."

"He was outside the Eagle's Nest during the reception for Olivia and Clay. It was for a few seconds, then he disappeared. I tried finding him, but couldn't. Figured I was mistaken. Still, I should've told you."

"Enoch remembered his name, so I went through the wanted posters. Didn't find one on him."

"He shot and killed a Texas Ranger, bank manager, and deputy. I was there when he shot the deputy. When Burris fired at me, his brother stepped between him and my bullet." Chan massaged the back of his neck. "An accountant. Didn't even carry a gun."

"He died?"

Chan nodded.

"It's taken him a while to track you down."

"*If* it was him. Maybe my memory is faulty."

"Is that what you believe?" Gabe asked.

"Right now, I don't know what I believe. Still, we should be cautious. If it is Burris, he won't care who gets hurt as long as he kills me."

Gabe glanced out the window at the still dark sky, absently stroking his jaw. "I'll send a telegram to your ex-captain asking for a copy of the wanted poster."

"I'll do that. Maybe Burris has been arrested in Texas, which means whoever I saw wasn't him."

"Your eyesight and instincts are excellent. If you believe you spotted Burris, you did. You'll be coming to the jail with me this morning."

"Already planned on it." Chan finished his coffee, stood, and paced to the window.

"You'll describe Burris to my deputies. Everyone will be watching for him."

"I'll find Enoch and get him to the jail. Nobody blends in better than him."

Gabe chuckled, thinking of the town drunk. To everyone's surprise, he'd been ready to take a bullet for

Caleb Covington when an outlaw came after the deputy. There was a lot more to Enoch Weaver than anyone expected.

"Good idea. What are you going to do about Agent Cartman?"

"Nothing I *can* do. I've been ordered to work with her, which I'll do."

"And your past?" Gabe asked.

Chan stared at the wall behind his brother, features remote. "What happened before has no impact on the investigation or my future. Elizabeth Cartman is just another woman." He strolled across the kitchen, glancing over his shoulder at Gabe before heading back to his room. "Nothing more."

Chapter Sixteen

Beth walked along the boardwalk, passing one shop after another. Most were closed this early in the morning, a good time for her to study the town without anyone bothering her—without Chan questioning her actions.

Splendor was bigger than she'd imagined, yet smaller than Big Pine. Betts, the owner of McCall's restaurant, told her at breakfast the town had tripled in size over the last two years. The Devil Dancer mine accounted for much of the growth, enticing travelers to stay, opening shops and restaurants or buying land to raise cattle.

Betts had been friendly and talkative, answering questions before Beth could ask them. The Pelletiers were the biggest landowners, running cattle and breeding horses. Suzanne and Nick Barnett, along with Gabe and Lena Evans, owned several successful businesses, which surprised her. She wondered about a sheriff having the money to build a fancy hotel and restaurant. It was easier for her to understand him having enough to partner in the Dixie and Wild Rose saloons.

Beth had learned to look for inconsistencies, question whatever didn't make sense. The scope of Gabe Evans's properties didn't add up. A sheriff's salary didn't support such lavish investments. So where did his money come from? Was it possible Chan's brother had gotten involved in illegal activities such as counterfeiting? They were questions she needed to have answered.

Taking a seat on a bench across the street from the jail, Beth was surprised when someone joined her. An older man in a rumpled suit, bow tie, and black derby hat, hands clasped in his lap, sat a foot away.

"I don't believe we've met. I'm Enoch Weaver."

A slight smile curved her lips. "Elizabeth Cartman. It's a pleasure to meet you."

"The pleasure is all mine, Miss Cartman. Are you new to Splendor?"

"I arrived yesterday from Big Pine with Marshal Evans."

"Chan. An excellent lawman and good person. You were fortunate to have him ride with you."

"Yes, I was," she whispered.

"Good morning." Both turned their attention to Chan, who stood a couple feet away. "I've been looking for you, Enoch."

"Seems you've found me, Marshal. What can I do for you?"

"Do you have time to join Gabe and me at the jail?"

"I've nowhere to go, so yes." Standing, Enoch tipped his derby hat at Beth. "It was nice to meet you, Miss Cartman."

She stood, glaring at Chan. "Does this have anything to do with the reason I came to Splendor? If so, I'm going with you."

Blowing out a sigh, he nodded. "Fine. It'll give you a chance to meet Gabe's deputies." He'd hoped to get through this meeting before locating Beth and starting their interviews.

And learn more about the sheriff. "Thank you."

Walking across the street, Chan shoved the door open, motioning them inside. Gabe, Beau, Cash, Hex, Zeke, and Caleb were already inside. Making introductions, he indicated for Beth to sit down.

"What about Mack and Dutch?" Chan asked.

"They should be here soon." Gabe turned his attention to Beth. "Good morning, Agent Cartman."

"Sheriff."

"I see you've met Enoch."

Her features softened when she looked at the older man. "Yes."

The door opened, Mack and Dutch entering. Both stopped when they saw her.

"Agent Cartman, this is Mack Mackey and Dutch McFarlin."

Removing their hats, each nodded in greeting.

"Gentlemen. Are these all your deputies, Sheriff?"

"Yes. Chan, why don't you start?"

An hour later, questions answered and plans made, Gabe ended the meeting. Each man had the same assignment—locate Burris and make discreet inquiries to assist Chan and Beth with their investigation.

Enoch would be doing his part by acting himself. The town drunk most people ignored. Chan, Gabe, and his deputies knew the truth. Underneath the pain he concealed with alcohol was a brilliant mind, one which had propelled him into the highest echelons of the courthouse in Cincinnati.

He'd shared little about what had caused him to leave it all behind, bury himself in the saloons of Splendor, but they assumed it had been some type of devastating loss.

"When were you planning on telling me about Burris?" Beth fumed as she walked alongside Chan on their way to the telegraph office.

"I'm still not sure Burris is the man I saw. Gabe is being cautious, nothing more."

"You're not being honest with me, Chan."

Stopping, he pinned her with a hard stare, backing her against the wall of a nearby shop. He leaned toward her, his mouth not more than six inches away. Too close. Yet not close enough.

"I'm not like you, Beth. I don't lie."

As much as she wanted to deny it, forget her feelings for the handsome lawman, she'd never gotten over him. Her mouth went dry, throat constricting, heart pounding in her chest. It was too much, more than she could deal with right now.

Placing her hands on his chest, Beth shoved. The action had no effect. "What is that supposed to mean? I've never lied to you."

"You haven't been honest, either, which is just as bad." He blew out a breath, taking a step away, his breathing more ragged than before. "I'll do what I can to help locate the forgers. In return, I expect to be provided with everything you've learned, not the bits and pieces you and Thad deem necessary."

Unable to meet his gaze, she took a step forward. "I don't know what you mean."

"Ah, Beth. You're such a bad liar." Turning on his heel, he continued toward the telegraph office, not caring if she followed or not.

Chan knew he didn't need her to discover illegal activities in Splendor involving fake bank notes. With the help of Gabe and his men, they'd run down every lead and discover if there was merit to the suspicions of the two agents.

"Chan, wait."

Whirling around, he crossed his arms. "What?"

Halting a foot away, she took a step back at the unconcealed anger on his face. Heart still racing, Beth jutted out her chin. She wouldn't allow him to intimidate her or treat her as if she weren't his equal.

"Not once did I lie to you in Austin, nor have I lied to you since."

"But you never told me everything, did you? Not then. Not now." Chan glared down at her, waiting for a response. When none came, he turned back around, his boots pounding on the boardwalk.

She didn't try to stop him this time, following not far behind. When he reached the telegraph office, Chan stopped.

"I'll do the talking. Bernie is a good man, but a little jumpy. He'll be friendly to you, but will *listen* to me." Opening the door, he stepped inside, leaving her on the boardwalk to fume or follow.

"Morning, Marshal. What can I do for you this morning?"

"Morning, Bernie. I just have some questions for you." Chan heard the door close, assuming Beth had decided to come inside.

Pushing his spectacles up his nose, Bernie set down his pencil. "I'll answer what I can."

Chan could already see his eyes dart around, hands tapping the counter. Signs the man was getting agitated. "Do you remember anyone bringing in a package showing *just* Splendor in the upper left corner?"

"Happens all the time, Marshal. Fact is, some don't have anything other than where the package is to go."

"Letters?"

"Same." Bernie's fingers tapped more rapidly on the counter, his gaze darting between Chan and Beth. "If I know them, I'll write their last name, and I always add Montana Territory if it's missing."

"Anyone you didn't recognize come in recently?"

"A few, when they get off the stage and want to post a letter before moving on." Bernie's body rose up and down in quick succession, indicating he bobbed on the balls of his feet. A sign he was becoming more disturbed.

Resting his hands on the counter, Chan leaned forward a little. Not enough to spook Bernie any further. "You're about the best postmaster I've ever known. I'd bet you'd notice anything that didn't make sense."

A smile broke across Bernie's face. "Sure thing, Marshal. I've been in this job since Splendor opened a telegraph and post office. Watched many comings and goings."

"I'm sure you've seen a lot that doesn't make sense."

Bernie cackled, relaxing a little. "A bit more than you'd think."

"Any odd happenings lately?"

"You mean the last week or so?"

"Longer. Maybe six months back?"

Pursing his lips, Bernie's fingers continued to drum on top of the counter. "Don't think so, Marshal." He paused a minute, scratching his stubbled chin. "Those Chinese have mailed a few more packages than normal, but not letters."

"Do you recall where the packages were sent?"

"Well now, let me think. As I remember, some went to Big Pine, maybe Kansas City, but I can't swear to it."

"When was the last time they mailed a package?"

"It's been a while, Marshal. A month maybe."

Straightening, Chan held out his hand, shaking Bernie's. "You've been a big help." Starting for the door, he stopped. "Let me know if anything odd happens or the Chinese mail another package."

Bernie touched the brim of his cap. "Will do, Marshal."

Passing Beth, he opened the door, indicating for her to step out ahead of him. Adjusting his hat, Chan started walking toward the area of Splendor known as Chinatown.

It had grown rapidly over the last couple years, made up of mine workers too old to continue the backbreaking work. As Chan recalled Gabe's story, a grocery opened first, followed by a laundry, boardinghouse, restaurants, herb shop, general store, meat market, and finally, a tiny bookstore, which sold pamphlets in their native language and published a Chinese newspaper. The latter was what kept the business going.

The last drew Chan's attention. Their newspaper had first been published in the last year, about the same time Beth and Thad believed shipments from Splendor began.

The pieces seemed to be falling into place.

Chapter Seventeen

"Where are we going?" Beth hurried to catch up to Chan, her strides shorter, necessitating her to increase her speed.

Chan didn't slow his pace. "Chinatown."

"What are we looking for?"

He glanced behind, seeing a slight gleam of moisture on her face. Stopping, Chan waited for her. "Anything to help your investigation."

"*Our* investigation, Chan."

Ignoring her, he continued toward the Chinese part of town, this time at a slower pace. He didn't want to antagonize her any further. They had a job to do. The sooner they determined if Splendor was a printing and distribution source for forged notes, the sooner she'd leave and he could return to his life.

For a split second, an image of Francesca O'Reilly crossed his mind. Curvy, with auburn hair and green eyes. Not the blonde hair and violet eyes of the woman next to him.

He guessed the two were about the same age, older than him, which didn't matter at all to Chan. Both were pretty, smart, had been born not far from him in New York. Why did one spark his desire and the other less so?

Before coming across Beth in Big Pine, he'd been prepared to see Francesca again, possibly court her to explore where a relationship might go. For now, he would let those thoughts go. Once Beth had returned east and he'd spent time back on Dom's ranch, he'd ask Francesca to supper.

Shaking thoughts of the two women from his mind, Chan stopped again. "Gabe told me about a printing press being delivered to one of the Chinese shops about a year ago. I want to see it for myself."

"I've never come across Chinese printing fake bills."

"Doesn't mean they can't. Who would suspect them, Beth?"

"No one. What are they using the press for now?"

"A Chinese newspaper, posters, books."

"Books?" Beth asked.

"Gabe told me they translate English books to Chinese. According to my brother, they're doing well."

"In such a small town as Splendor?"

Chan stopped at the corner where Chinatown began, glancing up and down the street. "They ship them all over."

"Did you ask the telegraph clerk about packages of their books?" Beth asked.

"No. I will if it appears they're printing something other than newspapers and books."

It made sense and was the best option they had right now. Bernie Griggs hadn't been much help. He might be jumpy, but seemed honest, and had been doing his job a long time. Whatever was going on in Splendor, it had nothing to do with the postmaster.

Chan walked past several stores, stopping outside the one he knew sold books. He opened the door. It was a miniscule space, perhaps ten feet across, but deep, close to thirty feet before a partition closed off what was in back.

Searching the shelves, they moved toward the partition, seeing nothing indicating illegal activities. Nor did they spot a printing press, although there were copies of the newspaper in stacks on the counter, an older issue than the pile sitting by the front door.

"Anyone here?" Chan called out while continuing to search the books, moving them aside to see if anything hid behind them.

"Yes. Yes." An older man came from the back, a weary expression on his face. "What you want?"

"I understand you print the Chinese newspaper."

The man looked between the two, settling his attention back on Chan. "Yes. You see." He picked up a copy of the single page paper, holding it out to him.

"May I see the press you use?"

The man's brows drew together. "Press?"

"Your printing press."

Hearing noises from the back, Chan looked past the man. Without asking permission, he moved around him.

"Wait. Wait." The man rushed after him, trying to tug on Chan's arm.

Shoving aside a curtain, he saw three other men huddled around a press, their eyes wide. They began talking at once, the shop owner joining in, motioning with his arms.

Chan took his time, bending down to check lower shelves, opening cupboards, pulling aside stacks of paper to peek behind them. Nothing.

Walking around the press, he continued to search, opening the door to look outside. Still nothing.

At first, Beth stayed in the front, checking again for anything out of place. Giving up, she followed Chan, stopping next to the press. Experience guided her in what to look for, what to ignore. No matter how cautious, every counterfeiter left clues. Tiny bits of paper used for printing notes, special cans of ink in different colors, plates hidden in remote places while still being accessible.

Acknowledging the plates could be hidden in the apartment upstairs or somewhere else, she found none of what she expected.

Meeting Chan's gaze, she shook her head. He returned the gesture, turning toward the older man.

"I appreciate you letting us look around, Mr..."

He paused a moment before answering. "Lee Yang."

"Mr. Yang, sorry if we disturbed you."

Yang didn't answer, choosing to usher them through the store and out the front door.

"I was certain we'd find something."

"It doesn't mean you were wrong, Chan. Because we didn't find anything this time doesn't mean they aren't the counterfeiters. Hiding ink, paper, and plates isn't that hard. They could be anywhere, possibly in the apartment above the shop."

"I'll give it a few days, then come by again."

"*We'll* come by again, Chan."

"Sure, Agent Cartman. Whatever you want."

Cullen Burris followed the marshal and woman to McCall's, staying close against the buildings so he wouldn't be spotted. He had no desire to call Evans out with a woman by his side, and since the marshal's return to town, they'd been together more than apart.

Burris needed to get him alone, away from town. A fair fight had never occurred to him. He was growing tired of the frontier town, and a quick end suited him fine.

Seeing them take a table at the back of the restaurant, he decided to go to the boardinghouse restaurant for lunch. He'd planned to take care of the marshal that morning and already be on a trail to other places. Burris didn't much care where. San Francisco maybe, or farther south. As long as it was too far away for anyone to come after him.

Ignoring the man in a suit, bow tie, and dusty, black derby hat, Burris glanced behind him. No sign of the marshal or woman. He didn't expect there to be, but by nature and profession, he was a cautious man.

Burris needed food and several cups of coffee to work through a plan to eliminate Evans without drawing attention to himself. Late at night in Chinatown made the most sense. The problem was getting him there, alone.

The marshal was far from a stupid man. In fact, he was as smart as his older brother, a faster gun, and quick to deliver justice. None of those boded well for the outlaw. He wasn't as young and had a slower draw.

Unlike Evans, Burris was ruthless, caring nothing about fair play. Drawing him into a dark alley in Chinatown made the most sense, unless the marshal rode back to the Lucero ranch. Killing him while on the trail north would be ideal. It could be days before that happened, and Burris didn't have a way to find out when that would be. No. Ambushing him in a dark alley would be best.

Cheyenne, Wyoming

Gyp Slade stretched, rolling to his back on the lumpy mattress in the tiny hotel room. His eyes refused to open, not wanting to feel the pain of bright sunlight streaming through the slits in the curtain.

Groaning, he rubbed his eyes, swinging his feet to the floor. He cursed himself for drinking so much the night before. At the time, each swallow felt good, the burn more soothing than irritating.

Standing with a groan, Gyp looked around the room, puzzled. He didn't remember climbing the stairs, removing his boots, or shrugging out of his clothes. All he could recall was drinking one shot after another, playing cards, and ignoring one of the working girls who refused to leave him alone. And he remembered Hugh and Harvey being at the same table.

Splashing water on his face, Gyp dressed, running hands through his hair. Glancing at the hook by the door, he stilled. His gunbelt was gone. He whirled around to check the bedstand. His gun was also gone.

No. It had to be in the room somewhere. He did a cursory check of the room, not finding the gunbelt or gun.

Swearing, Gyp slammed his hat down on his head and left his room. The smell of bacon and eggs wafted up the stairwell. His stomach rumbled. He had a decision to make. Eat and satisfy the hunger, or find his gun. Food could wait. Locating his gun couldn't.

Reaching the lobby, he walked to the clerk's desk. "Did my friends leave anything for me?"

The man seemed perplexed. "Are you looking for anything specific, Mr. Slade?"

Patience wasn't a strength of his. "My gun."

"Oh, surely not, but I'll check." Rising, he walked around a wall to what Gyp knew was a supply room.

He could hear the door creak open and close before the clerk reappeared a couple minutes later. "I'm sorry, but we don't have your gun, Mr. Slade."

"You're certain?"

"Yes, sir."

His jaw clenched in an attempt to tamp down his frustration. "Have you seen my companions this morning?"

"The Fisher brothers? They left early this morning, maybe four hours ago."

"Left?"

"Yes, sir. Paid for last night, including your room, and said they wouldn't be back. Their saddlebags appeared packed to travel."

Blowing out a harsh curse, Gyp ignored the way the clerk winced and took a step backward.
"Did they say where they were going?"

He gave a short shake of his head, voice shaky. "No, sir. They ate early and left."

Rage rolled through him, enough he wanted to slam his fist onto the desk. The gesture would accomplish nothing except encourage the clerk to find the sheriff or a deputy. He didn't need a lawman in his business or slowing down his search for Hugh and Harvey.

Harvey had tested Gyp's patience from the time they met. He ignored the subtle insults because of the man's expertise with a gun and total lack of fear. He liked Hugh. The brother had a quick mind and mild manner, not prone to rash decisions. A peacemaker was how Gyp thought of him.

Now he saw both as men who'd betrayed him. The Fishers had to be the ones who hauled him to his room. They took his gun, paid his bill, and rode out without him.

Gyp hadn't expected it. Maybe from Harvey, but not Hugh.

"Mr. Slade?"

He looked up at the clerk.

"There is this message for you. The clerk at the telegraph office brought it by earlier." He held out the telegram, drawing his hand away when Gyp snatched it.

He walked away, reading slowly, which was his normal pace. The outlaw was proficient with guns, excellent at carrying out assignments. He'd never been a man of letters or numbers.

Stopping, he read the short message again, making certain he had the meaning right. Priest had changed the next assignment. Instead of stopping the stage between Big Pine and Moosejaw, they'd be raiding it between Splendor and the territorial capital. It left Gyp with a real problem.

He had a week to ride north and no men to go with him. Three was the minimum needed to complete the assignment for Simon. Gyp had no choice but to locate two or three new partners, a job he didn't have time to accomplish to his satisfaction.

Folding the telegram, he crammed it into a pocket and walked into the dining room. He had two options. One, search for men in Cheyenne, or two, wait until he reached Splendor. Neither felt right.

Sitting down, he ordered eggs, bacon, sausage, and several biscuits, along with a cup of coffee, before leaning back in his chair. He did his best thinking with a full stomach.

Gyp recalled two men he'd seen in the saloon several times. Younger than him, hungry looking, with hard eyes and guns fastened low on their waists. He was certain they weren't ranch hands.

These men were tough, gazes distant, not men who stayed in one place long. Then he recalled one wearing a well-worn cap of a Confederate soldier. It was the last that made up his mind.

Forking the last piece of sausage into his mouth, Gyp finished his coffee, paid, and headed out. He had a lot to do, and a short period of time to do it.

Chapter Eighteen

Beth held the wine glass to her lips, giving her a moment to watch Chan without him noticing. She'd always thought him more rugged than handsome. Over the weeks they were together, Beth had come to admire everything about him.

Chocolate brown eyes which turned umber when making love or angry. His dark brown hair showed streaks of gold when he stood in the sun. Chan had a wicked sense of humor and quick mind. According to Captain Jones, he was a superb Texas Ranger, a man you could depend on, never wonder about his dedication.

When his eyes met hers, she took a sip of wine, setting down the glass. They'd ordered supper, and on the server's recommendation, two slices of May Covington's fresh berry pie. Beth knew there were things they needed to say, answers to his angry assertions earlier in the day.

Though she hadn't lied to him, she'd held back information which might help them in their search. Knowledge which hadn't seemed important earlier. Now it did. Before she could speak, Chan leaned forward, his question not at all what she expected.

"Why did you leave? The truth, Beth."

She felt as if he'd slapped her, which was no less than she deserved. Leaving him with a brief note, no reasons, no apology, had been wrong, a mistake Beth could never rectify. And she desperately wanted to correct what she'd done, beseech his forgiveness. Instead, she found herself closing up, pride stopping honesty.

"It's simple. I wasn't over my husband's death." Her hand shook as she picked up her wine glass. She took several sips before setting it down, grasping the stem to hide her trembling fingers. The instant her eyes locked with his, she knew it had been a wasted effort.

"You mean you felt *guilty* about falling in love. It was easier to leave." He waited until the server set plates in front of them and left. "Then there was the issue of me being four years younger than you. I cared nothing about it. To you, it meant a great deal." Chan picked up his fork, shrugging. "You weren't as strong as I'd thought."

Chest constricting at the truth of his words, her breaths changed to short gasps. Fisting her hands, Beth kept them concealed in her lap while regaining her composure.

He was right. She'd been a coward in so many ways. Not once had she talked of her reservations, while Chan had been honest, hiding nothing. Beth knew she'd fallen in love, but had kept her feelings buried.

"If I could go back, do it all differently, I would. And yes, I was a coward. Scared of what I felt, of what it could lead to, of the possibility, as years passed, you'd find someone younger."

Setting down his fork, he studied her. At last, the truth. "I loved you, Beth. The age difference didn't matter to me. Four years is nothing. My sister, Nora, is married to Wyatt Jackson. He's three years younger. They're very happy, planning to have children soon."

"Was she a widow, too?"

"No, but both Caro Davis and Isabella Dixon were widows when they arrived in Splendor. Both are married and happy. I'll be glad to introduce you to any of them." Chan stayed silent while the server removed their supper dishes, filled coffee cups, and placed large slices of pie in front of them. "Are you still in love with Abner?"

Beth jerked enough for Chan to notice, forgetting she'd told him about Abner's work, and the details of his death. "No. But I'll always hold him close in my heart and will never forget him."

Her answer was enough to give him hope.

"Why do you ask about him, Chan?"

He chewed the last bite of pie, washing the berry confection down with coffee. Letting the question settle for a few moments, he reached over, settling his hand over hers.

"Because, this time, you aren't leaving without a proper goodbye, Beth."

Burris sat inside McCall's, finishing a meal of roast beef and potatoes. He'd seen Chan and the woman go into the St. James Hotel, watched through the windows of the Eagle's Nest as they sat down for supper.

The couple had completed dessert, sipping coffee while they talked. Burris watched the marshal place his hand over the woman's. He smiled at the knowledge Evans cared about her more than as a colleague. Good information. If he couldn't get him alone, the outlaw would consider using the woman as bait.

Leaning back in the chair, he picked up his coffee, sipping as he continued to watch them. He took his time, the same as they were doing. Burris felt no sense of urgency. For now, he was content filling in pieces of the marshal's life. Brother of the sheriff, possible lover of the woman with him in the Eagle's Nest.

From the few conversations he'd overheard about Evans, people liked and respected him, the same as his brother, Gabe. Their sister, Nora, had married a Pelletier ranch hand and worked for the woman who owned the dress shop and millinery. Lots of people to use as bait to draw the marshal out.

Burris rocked back in the chair, a feral smile tipping the corners of his mouth. Evans had made a mistake, moving to a town with people he cared about.

He thought of his own brother, a quiet, unassuming accountant who'd never hurt anyone. His only mistake had been to follow Burris the night the Texas Ranger spotted him. Instead of the outlaw lying in the dirt, it had been a younger, much better version of himself.

Burris hadn't grieved the loss of their parents. They'd been old, worn out, ready to finish hard lives of grueling work with little reward. He had mourned the death of his brother.

The idea came to him in a moment of complete clarity. Instead of going after Evans, he'd kill the sheriff, create the same pain the marshal had given Burris. Afterward, he'd still go after Chan Evans, but he'd have the satisfaction of seeing agony on the man's face, the same as the outlaw had experienced.

Chan followed Beth up the stairs to the second floor of the St. James Hotel. Neither spoke as they approached her room. Propriety decreed he not go inside.

Stopping at the door, Beth unlocked it and turned to look at him. "Would you—"

"Yes." He moved toward her, taking her shoulders to guide her inside, then kicked the door closed. Wrapping an arm around her waist, Chan drew Beth to him, covering her mouth with his.

The response was immediate. Her reticule slipped from her hand to the floor, arms circling his neck, drawing him down.

Mutual desire flamed the passion each had ignored, flaring to life. Tongues tangling, hands moving over each other at a frantic pace. Bending, he swept her into his arms.

Hers was a large room with a big, soft bed, perfect for what Chan planned. As hard as it would be, he'd take his time, making love to Beth over hours, not minutes, letting her know how much he desired her. Age played no part between them, and by the time morning came, Chan would have her believing it.

Beth burrowed under the covers, a hand splaying across Chan's chest, her leg covering his. A deep sigh left her lips as fingers explored his upper body. A soft chuckle had her looking up.

Chan stared down at her, eyes darkening. A broad, calloused hand smoothed over her back, sending chills of desire through her. He wanted her again, and she wanted him, but there was no time.

"I should go." His deep, rough voice flowed through her. She still couldn't believe Chan was with her after all this time. Beth also didn't know where they'd go from here, if anywhere.

"It wouldn't do for you to be seen leaving my room."

Brushing hair off her forehead, he gently rolled off the bed and stood. Dressing, he strapped on his gunbelt, walking around to Beth's side and sitting down.

"I'll come by early to escort you to breakfast. We can talk about what we'll do next."

"All right." She hoped he'd say more, such as the night had been wonderful and he wanted more. She saw no hint of the lover from only an hour before.

Touching her bare shoulder, he stroked fingers down her arm, then stood. "I'll see you in a few hours."

A chill sliced through her at the sound of the door closing. He'd made no promises of seeing her again beyond their assignment.

What she did remember was him telling her he expected a proper goodbye when she left. Sitting up, she yanked the blanket to cover her chest, staring out the window to the dark, cloudless sky.

The night they'd shared had meant nothing to him. A few hours of pleasure and he'd gotten what he wanted. When the assignment finished, he'd expect her to leave so he could get back to his regular life.

Being a U.S. Marshal suited him. The rancher part surprised Beth. He was a city boy from New York, leaving because he hadn't fit his parents' idea of becoming a success. Banking, finance, accounting, politics—any of those would've been more appropriate than becoming a Texas Ranger, a marshal, or a rancher. He'd followed his older brother's path, riding west and becoming a lawman.

Beth hadn't noticed the moisture in her eyes until a tear trailed down her cheek. Angry at the perceived weakness, she swiped it off her face and threw off the covers. Stomping to the wardrobe, she grabbed a nightdress and slipped into it.

Hours before dawn, she went through the morning ritual of washing her face and brushing her hair. Staring at herself in the mirror, Beth felt a hollowness in her chest, pressure around her heart.

Running fingers through her long tresses, she forced her thoughts away from Chan to the assignment. The sooner they solved the case, the sooner she could be on her way home to a small, quiet, sparsely furnished apartment not far from headquarters. To the life she'd chosen. The only life she knew.

Cheyenne, Wyoming

Gyp swung atop his horse, waiting as the other two men did the same. In their early twenties and enthusiastic, they were his new partners, ready to do whatever he asked for the promised money.

He'd talked to them over two days, taken them out of town to study their skills with a weapon. Not as good as Harvey, but better than Hugh. One more contemplative, the other less so. He reminded himself they had to get through the latest orders from Simon, then Gyp could decide if they were the kind of men who could ride with him for more assignments.

They didn't know the goal consisted of assisting the distribution of forged notes. The job included robbing a stage, nothing more. It was all they'd learn until well afterward.

It would take a few days to reach Splendor. The change in the orders made no sense to Gyp. In the past, they received the packages in Big Pine or Moosejaw and took them to Denver to start the second part of their journey.

This meant repackaging the notes, sending them east and south. Rarely were they shipped west. The recipients would pass some of the bills around, shipping the rest to predesignated locations.

Within a few days, Gyp's fee would be sent to his bank. He'd split it between his two new partners, then the cycle would start again. He didn't know if they were one of a few or one of many who performed this work. As long as he got paid, Gyp didn't care.

The three men rode north. He'd already told them to keep watch for two men, describing Hugh and Harvey. If they saw them, his new partners were to shoot to kill, asking no questions. Neither flinched at the order.

One excellent opportunity came from the change in plans. Gyp would have a chance to locate and kill one of a handful of men in Montana who could cut his job short. A job he hoped to keep for a very long time.

U.S. Marshal Chan Evans may not have seen his face when they freed Simon from the Big Pine jail. Still, taking chances wasn't the way Gyp chose to work. Once he believed someone was a threat, he did what he could to stop them. He'd deal with the marshal as he had with others. Locate, kill him, and complete his orders.

Chapter Nineteen

Beth didn't take the seat next to Chan in the Eagle's Nest. Instead, she chose to sit across the table during breakfast. Better able to watch while far enough away so she wouldn't be tempted to touch him.

He didn't acknowledge her decision or seem to care. Chan ate while they discussed the day's activities. They'd seen nothing in the Chinese bookshop to prove they were printing anything except their newspaper. That left one other printing press in town.

Lewis Gibson and his son, Franklin, wrote and distributed the Splendor Herald from their small shop between the Dixie and the emporium owned by Dom Lucero's wife, Josie, and her good friend, Olivia Barnett McCord.

The paper came out once a week, unless there was a story of urgent interest. The father and son had been in Splendor a few years, and Chan couldn't find a reason why they'd be involved in any illegal activities.

"Are you ready to talk to the Gibsons?" Chan stood, not moving to pull out her chair. It was as if she were staring at a stranger rather than the man who'd made passionate love to her the night before.

Shoving her chair out, Beth stood, leaving the restaurant without looking at him.

"Beth, wait."

She didn't. He'd been cold and distant since entering the Eagle's Nest, and she'd had enough of it. Not bothering to wait for him to catch up, she walked past the emporium, stopping in front of the newspaper office.

"Beth, about last night—"

She held up her hand, halting whatever else he meant to say. "It was nice, Chan. Now, are you ready to speak with the Gibsons?"

He didn't move. "Nice?"

Touching his arm, her lips twisted into a mischievous grin. "Maybe a little better than nice." When she reached out to grab the doorknob, he clenched her wrist.

"It was a whole lot better than nice, Beth."

She pulled her wrist free. "Was it?" This time, she turned the knob, entering to the sound of a press doing its job.

"Well, hello there, Marshal. It's good to see you." Lewis Gibson walked toward them, hand extended.

"Mr. Gibson. This is Miss Elizabeth Cartman, a friend of mine from back east."

"It's a pleasure, Miss Cartman."

She offered a honeyed smile. "Mr. Gibson."

"What brings the two of you in here this morning?"

"Miss Cartman has an interest in newspapers and how they're printed. I thought you might have a few minutes to show her around."

Gibson's face brightened. "It would be a pleasure."

While the editor showed Beth around, Chan explored on his own, even poking his head into the back room. Gibson's son, Franklin, busied himself setting type.

"Good morning, Franklin."

Chan's voice startled the young man. He dropped the tray of type on the floor, the contents scattering. Crouching down, he helped Franklin return the pieces to the tray, then stood.

"Didn't mean to surprise you."

Slender, shy, and as pale as winter snow, Franklin's hands shook as he organized the type. He looked more like an older boy than a young man.

"It's fine. I was concentrating on my work."

"Are you preparing this week's paper?"

"Yes." His voice shook enough for Chan to notice.

Glancing around the small space, he didn't see anything suspicious, the same as in Chinatown. It made him wonder if somewhere in Splendor another press had been delivered and hidden away. If not, it meant Thad and Beth's information was incorrect and the notes were not coming from town. The return address had been a way to throw people off, turn attention away from where the notes were printed and distributed.

"I'll let you get back to your work, Franklin."

"Good to see you, Marshal."

Chan walked back to the front. Beth and Lewis were engaged in an intense conversation as he explained how the newspaper business worked. He found it amusing.

She probably knew much more than Gibson about printing from her work hunting down counterfeiters. Still, her face showed a deep interest in every word.

"It's all fascinating, Mr. Gibson. Have you been doing this a long time?"

"My entire life. Started out in my hometown of Kansas City. We moved here a couple years after the war ended."

"I went through Kansas City on my way here," Beth said.

"For a long time, at the start of the war, we thought the Confederates would win. Didn't turn out that way." His voice had turned solemn, almost bitter.

"You supported the South?" Beth asked.

He shrugged. "Like a lot of people, I had family in the South. Georgia and Mississippi. By the time it was over, they'd lost everything."

Beth had heard the same story many times. No matter how often, the misery the war caused always made her stomach roil.

"It appears you made a good decision to come here."

"I agree, Miss Cartman."

"Are you ready?" Chan moved next to her, resting a hand on the small of her back, feeling her flinch.

"Yes. Thank you again, Mr. Gibson. You've been quite informative."

"You're welcome to come back anytime, Miss Cartman. My son and I are here every day except Sunday."

Stepping outside, they walked several feet before Beth spoke. "Did you see anything suspicious?"

"Nothing. Mr. Yang and Gibson are the only two who have presses in Splendor."

"Are you certain?"

"I already spoke to Gabe about it. He's only aware of two, but has told his deputies to ask questions, find out if there is another one."

She knew what it meant if no other presses were found. Either they'd missed something or the return address had been a ruse, meant to send them in the wrong direction. A clever way to throw people off their trail.

"What do we do now?"

Chan continued along the boardwalk, crossing the street toward the telegraph office. "You're going to send a telegram to Thad telling him we've found nothing."

His meaning was clear. Chan felt they'd done all they could and found nothing. He was ready to return to his life and send her back east to hers. As much as she wanted to argue, Beth couldn't. Nor would she stay if he didn't want her.

It took little time to send the short message to Thad. Returning outside, she glanced up and down the street, spotting a man she'd noticed watching them more than once.

"Do you know the man standing outside the Land Office?"

Chan's attention shot across the street, but no one was there. "What man?"

Beth stepped to the edge of the boardwalk, blinking. The man was gone. "There was someone there, Chan. I've seen him watching us more than once."

Grabbing her arm, he tugged her back toward the building, moving in front of her. "What did he look like?"

"A little heavyset. Under six feet tall, brown hat, and a pair of six-shooters at his waist."

"Burris."

Her brows rose. "The gunfighter from Austin?"

"The description fits. You should've told me about seeing him earlier."

"I didn't know who he was, just that he was watching us."

Taking her elbow, Chan guided her into the jail, indicating a chair. Gabe sat at his desk, scanning a ledger. Probably from one of his numerous businesses.

"Beth saw Burris."

Shoving the ledger aside, Gabe narrowed his gaze on her. "Where?"

"Outside the Land Office. I saw the same man inside McCall's last night. I didn't know it was Burris."

"How long ago was he at the Land Office?"

"Ten minutes."

Seconds later, Gabe strode out the door, motioning to Caleb and Mack, who sat outside.

"Come with me." Gun in hand, he ran across the street, his deputies right behind him.

"Stay here, Beth."

"I'm going with you." She tried to move past Chan, but he shackled her arm in the biting grip of his strong hand.

"This has nothing to do with your case. It's about me and Burris." When she tried to pull from his grasp, he tugged her toward the back, grabbing the keys from a hook.

Fighting him, her eyes grew wide at the sight of the cells. "What are you doing?"

"I don't have time to argue and need to know you're safe." Opening the door, he shoved her inside a cell, locking it behind her.

Face red with anger, she gripped the bars. "You can't do this."

"I already did."

Hurrying off, he left a screaming Beth behind. There'd be hell to pay when he returned, but for now, she'd be safe.

Rushing outside, he crossed the street, seeing Caleb and Mack, guns drawn, standing at the outside corners of the Land Office. Gabe wasn't with them.

Before he caught up with them, a shot rang out behind the building. Not taking time to think, he ran, hearing another shot. Reaching the back of the building, Chan held his gun in front of him and peeked around the corner.

Gabe slumped against the back door of the Land Office, blood forming on his chest, his gun on the ground.

"Gabe!" Chan reached his side, barely noticing Caleb and Mack close by. Putting an arm around him, he helped him to the ground. His brother's shirt was already covered in red.

"Get the doctor," he yelled at the deputies, using his hands to try and stop the flow of blood.
"Don't you die on me, Gabe."

He continued the pressure, cursing and praying, his chest tight with fear. Taking a quick glance around, he didn't see Burris. A moment later, several townsfolk clustered around him, wide eyes staring down at the sheriff.

"Let me through." Clay McCord's voice came from the back of the crowd. Dropping his bag, he knelt next to Gabe. "Move aside, Marshal."

Chan didn't budge, continuing to apply pressure. Clay's voice hardened.

"Get on his other side. I need to see the wound and stop the bleeding." He worked for several minutes, muttering to himself. "The bullet went through. We need to get him to the clinic."

"We've got him, Doc." Beau Davis bent down, Cash, Caleb, and Mack joining him.

"Careful, boys," Clay admonished, watching as they lifted Gabe. Grabbing his bag, Clay began to follow when Chan gripped his arm.

“Will he make it, Doc?”
“I don’t know, Chan. I honestly don’t know.”

Chapter Twenty

Chan, Beth, and Lena sat with Walter Evans in the front room of the clinic, waiting for word of Gabe's condition. Beau had left to get Nora Evans Jackson and Nick and Suzanne Barnett, while Cash went to fetch Gabe's closest friend, Noah Brandt, and his wife, Abby. The other deputies guarded the town and watched for Cullen Burris.

The entire town was quiet, shocked at the attack on their sheriff. He'd always seemed invincible, a man able to overcome all obstacles. Now he fought for his life.

Both doctors, McCord and Worthington, tended to Gabe, yet neither had emerged with news. Chan didn't know if that was good or bad. Unable to sit still, he jumped up and paced across the expanse of the front room, stopping at the door to where his brother lay. He fought the urge to turn the knob and walk inside.

"He's going to be all right, son."

Chan stilled at his father's voice. He'd been a hard man, insisting his sons do what was proper, socially correct. After the death of his longtime mistress, a woman he'd loved his entire life, he'd softened somewhat. The news he also had a grown daughter, Nora, from their union stunned many, but enabled him to get closer to his oldest and youngest sons. Gabe and Chan had never judged him.

"How do you know?"

"Because I can't imagine a life without him." Walter placed a hand on Chan's shoulder and squeezed. "And because he has yet to see his baby born."

Lena was due to deliver any week. Chan glanced toward her, noting the sallow complexion, the way she clasped her hands so tight her knuckles had turned white. She was an intelligent, strong woman, yet today, Lena looked fragile, ready to shatter if the news was bad.

Nora joined them, her eyes red, skin pale. "I hate waiting."

Walter draped an arm around his only daughter. "We have to believe Gabe will make it, sweetheart." He kissed her forehead, tugging Nora into his side. "Zeke Boudreaux rode out to the Pelletier ranch to get Wyatt and let Dax and Luke know what happened."

As the words left his lips, the front door opened. Wyatt Jackson, Nora's husband, and Dax Pelletier walked in, striding directly to them. Nora went into Wyatt's arms.

"Any word?" Dax asked.

"Both doctors are with him. It's been almost two hours," Walter said, unable to hide the worry in his voice.

Dax glanced behind him at Lena. "Is there anything I can do?"

Walter shook his head. "No, but we're glad you're here."

"Do you know who did this?" Dax's question was directed to Chan.

"A killer named Cullen Burris."

The front door opened again. This time, Nick and Suzanne rushed inside, joining them by the examination room. Walter and Chan offered what they knew, which wasn't much before the Barnetts sat next to Lena.

When the exam room door opened, all eyes went to Clay McCord. Face drawn, expression conveying his deep concern, he stepped toward Lena.

"The bullet went straight through, but he's lost a lot of blood." Kneeling before her, he took her hands in his. "Right now, there's no way to know if he'll make it. We'll be better able to determine his prognosis after twenty-four hours. I'm sorry I don't have better news, Lena."

A sob broke from her lips before she could stop it. Beside her, Suzanne wrapped an arm around her closest friend.

Standing, Clay looked at the rest of the people holding a vigil for Gabe. "You know we'll do everything we can. Infection is our biggest enemy right now."

"May I see my son, Doctor?"

"For a minute, Mr. Evans, but no more. I'm certain Lena will want a minute, as well."

Chan stood a foot away. He didn't need to see Gabe to know what had to be done. Without a word, he stormed from the clinic, heading to the jail.

No one was inside. All the deputies were on the streets, searching for Burris. He planned to do the same, but alone.

Chan hadn't expected Burris to go after his brother. He'd underestimated the killer, should've thought it through. An eye for an eye. One brother for another.

Rage surged through him, which he ruthlessly tamped down. It wouldn't help to allow emotions to take over when he needed calm logic.

"He's staying at a rundown cabin south of town." Enoch Weaver met Chan as he walked out of the building.

"How do you know?"

"I followed him." Enoch sounded as if he did this all the time, when everyone knew he didn't own a horse. "It isn't that far. I thought it might be useful at some point."

"Come on." Chan ran toward the livery. Noah was at the clinic, so he ran straight for the stables in back. Tacking Caesar took little time. Same with a horse for Enoch.

Chan swung into his saddle while Enoch struggled a little before landing atop the gelding.

"Show me."

They reached the cabin in less than ten minutes. Stopping a decent distance away, they dismounted, Chan drawing his gun. To his surprise, Enoch pulled one from the inside pocket of his coat.

"Don't worry. I know how to use it."

"Stay here while I check the cabin." Chan didn't see a horse, which meant nothing.

"He rides a black stallion."

Chan nodded, then moved to the cabin, keeping himself hidden behind trees and bushes. He bent down, ran to the side of the building and looked inside. No one. Moving to the front, he peeked through the front window. He saw no one inside.

Frustrated, he entered anyway. If Enoch said Burris stayed here, then the outlaw did. Chan found nothing to indicate anyone had been inside in a long time.

Chan stalked back to Enoch and mounted Caesar. He didn't know where to go next, but it was just a matter of time before someone spotted Burris.

Shooting Gabe may have sated the outlaw's need to invoke pain on Chan. It didn't satisfy the man's goal of killing the lawman who'd fired the fatal shot.

Milwaukee, Wisconsin

Simon boarded the train, ready for his trip to Montana. He'd established what he considered an excellent crew of coney dealers, men and women who would pass the notes around for an agreed upon percentage.

Gyp had responded to the telegram Simon had sent from Milwaukee with the change in plans. Since no one had seen him or his two men, Hugh and Harvey, when they broke Simon out of the Big Pine jail, it was safer for him to go to Splendor. He trusted Gyp to meet with the counterfeiters in the frontier town, make certain they were happy.

It wouldn't be long before Damien had perfected the newest plates for shipment to their printers. He'd been an artist since he was a boy, always traveled with a pad of art paper and pencils. After the loss of his leg, he'd turned his talent into a lucrative profession. Not only did their illegal activities provide them with wealth beyond their imaginings, it added to the coffers of those Confederates who'd never given up the dream of independence. Someday, they planned another war, one they would win.

The Priest brothers ran a different operation from others who dealt in fake notes. They'd decided from the start to separate each step of the process, keeping their real identities secret from almost all those they hired.

Damien designed and created all the plates, which were sent to the printers. Simon established coney dealers to create multiple levels of distribution, as well as handled getting supplies to the printers. It was a lot more work, but provided the brothers with several layers of protection. It had worked well for almost five years.

Watching out the window, he closed his eyes and relaxed. He'd already sent a telegram to Damien, letting him know of his progress. His only job now was to go straight to Denver, get a room at the best hotel, eat a thick steak, and wait for word from Gyp.

Chan, Nick, and Gabe's deputies had scoured the town in their search for Burris, without luck. The man had disappeared as if he'd never existed.

Enoch rode back and forth to the cabin three times until it became too dark to see the trail. Burris hadn't reappeared. There was speculation he'd left the area. Most didn't believe it. Chan was certain the gunman had found another place to hide, biding his time until he could kill him.

Not once did Chan believe Burris would confront him in a fair fight. Shooting someone in the back without warning was more effective than calling a man out.

A few picked at suppers provided by Suzanne as they continued their vigil at the clinic. Others paced or spoke in small groups. Lena, Walter, Nora, and Chan took turns sitting next to Gabe, who had yet to awaken.

There'd been no sign of infection, the biggest risk at this point. If he made it through the night and the next day, his chances of recovering were excellent.

Isabella and Travis Dixon had volunteered to stay with Jack at the Evans' home. It had been an easy decision since Isabella had acted as his guardian for several years after Jack's birth.

"I should ride out." Chan stood with Zeke, Caleb, and Mack, the three deputies he felt closest to. "It's me he wants, not anyone else."

"Gabe wouldn't want you to make yourself a target," Caleb said. "If you leave here, you'll have several of us with you."

"No. I won't put any of you in danger."

Mack gave a mirthless chuckle. "It's not your decision."

Chan crossed his arms, glaring at them. "You can't stop me."

That had the three deputies laughing, drawing the attention of several others.

"Dutch, Cash, and Hex are making rounds, but Beau is at the jail," said Mack. "I'm certain he wouldn't mind having company."

Caleb shot a look at the exam room. "Don't do anything tonight, Chan. My guess is he's holed up for the night. Burris will know we're looking for him, so another attack won't come tonight."

Zeke leveled his hard gaze on Chan. "Your family needs to know you aren't in danger. They have enough to deal with. Don't make them worry about you, too."

Chan knew they were right, but his craving to act fought the logic of staying safe. He looked beyond them to Beth. She'd eaten little, preferring to help Suzanne bring meals over from the boardinghouse and get anything the others needed. When not helping, she sat away from the others, observing rather than getting further involved.

He appreciated her help, knew they had to talk soon and work out whatever was going on between them.

What happened the night before came as a surprise. Chan had never thought they'd be together again, and he wasn't sure they were now. He wished he had the right to take her in his arms, accept the comfort only Beth could provide. Instead, he'd stayed away, not wanting to expose his weakness for the beautiful Secret Service agent.

Chan hadn't been kind to Beth since leaving her bed. He'd seen the hurt on her face at his words and actions, yet she'd said nothing. Instead, he'd felt her pull away, determined to forget what they shared last night. He had no intention of letting her.

"Excuse me." Leaving the group, he dragged a chair next to her, resting a hand over hers.

"Thank you for helping Suzanne."

She shrugged, trying to remove her hand from under his. Chan didn't allow it. "I'm glad I had the chance to help."

They remained silent for several long moments before Chan spoke again. "This will delay our investigation."

"For now, this is more important. Besides, I can continue speaking with people without you. I still need to send a telegram to Thad about our progress."

"He may order you back."

"He might, but I hope not."

"No? I'm surprised you'd want to stay any longer than necessary."

Beth turned her hand over, lacing her fingers with his. "It's not so bad here. You have a lot of wonderful friends, people who genuinely care about you and your family. Unlike many back east, they're honest, people you can trust."

Squeezing her hand, he followed her gaze. "I came here to find Gabe. It wasn't my intention to stay longer than a few weeks. Then I accepted the marshal position and Dom offered me work on his ranch. No place has ever felt this right."

Blowing out a slow breath, she nodded. "I understand."

He placed a finger under her chin, lifting it so she met his gaze. "There's one thing missing, Beth."

Heart pounding, she felt her breath hitch. "What's that?"

"The woman I *still* love."

Chapter Twenty-One

Beth blinked, not once, but twice as Chan's hand tightened on hers. "The woman you still love?"

"I never lied to you about my feelings. Not in Austin, and not now."

Feeling heat flush her face, she squirmed in the chair, her tongue thick.

"You don't have to respond, Beth. It's probably best you don't. When the investigation is over, you'll go home and I'll be staying here."

The slight amount of hope she'd felt began slipping away. Chan might love her, but he wasn't willing to fight for her, try talking her into staying.

"I see." Sliding her hand from his, she shifted away before he could see her disappointment.

"Beth…"

She waited a moment until realizing he wasn't going to continue. "I do understand. You'd much prefer a woman who lives here, a quiet, sweet person who'll always agree with what you say, do everything you want." Beth didn't realize her voice rose with each sentence. Chan did. "No matter how much I love you, I'll never be that woman."

Standing, he gripped her arm, tugging Beth up. Ignoring her slight gasp and the stares of others, he guided her into an empty room. Shutting the door, he cupped her face with both hands, staring into eyes wide with surprise.

"You *love* me?"

Swallowing the uncertainty clogging her throat, she nodded. "Yes."

Not even a second passed before his mouth came down on hers. Deepening the kiss, his hands slid to Beth's back, drawing her against his chest as her arms circled his neck.

Last night had been wonderful, unexpected, with no assurance of more. This was different. As she melted against him, Chan couldn't help believing they were making a promise to each other of a possible future.

A soft knock on the door had him reluctantly ending the kiss.

"Chan?" He recognized Caleb's voice. "Gabe's awake."

Lena held Gabe's hand as Walter, Nora, and Chan clustered around the bed. Neither doctor expected him to be lucid for long, although both were pleased with his progress in such a short time.

He'd said one word since gaining consciousness. *Lena.* Gabe had repeated it over and over in a rough, pained voice until his eyes closed and he drifted away again.

"He's not quite over the risky period. Infection is still a possibility, but the fact he woke up so soon after getting wounded is an excellent sign." Charles Worthington, the older of the two doctors and founder of the clinic, placed a hand on Lena's shoulder. "His stubborn nature may be what saves him."

The uncle of Rachel Pelletier, everyone liked and respected Doc Worthington, considered him a leader in the community. He also never gave false hope. For him to say Gabe's progress was good brought a large measure of hope to those around the bed.

A minute later, he'd chased everyone out except Lena. When Gabe woke again, the doctor wanted hers to be the face he saw.

Chan ignored the puzzled expressions of those he passed on his way to Beth. Holding out a hand, he helped her up. "I need to get out of here for a little bit. Would you like to walk with me? Go to McCall's for pie and coffee before Betts closes?"

Biting her lower lip, she glanced out at the dark sky. "Yes, but I don't think it's such a good idea. Burris could be waiting for you."

She was right, which meant Beth would be in as much danger as him. He'd never knowingly put her at risk.

"How about I go to McCall's and have her wrap two slices of pie for us?"

"You aren't going out there alone, Beth." What Chan wanted was time alone with her, the pie being an enticement, but not the reason for the walk. "I'll ask Caleb to take you back to the hotel."

Beth's shoulders slumped for an instant before she straightened, hiding her disappointment. "All right."

Ignoring Chan's offer, she walked around him, stopping in front of the group of Gabe's deputies, looking at Caleb. "Would you have time to walk me back to the St. James?"

Brows furrowed, he shot a glance at Chan, who gave a terse nod. "Of course. Are you ready to leave now?"

"I am." Following him to the door, she stepped outside, drawing in a deep breath. The cool night air felt good, clearing her head. "Is May still working at the restaurant?"

Not looking at her, he focused his attention up and down the street, watching for anything that didn't fit. "She's home with our son, Isaac."

"You have a son? How wonderful. How old is he?"

"Three and a half. Isaac thinks he's much older, though." They crossed the main street toward the hotel. "You and Chan?"

Stumbling at his question, Caleb grabbed an arm, steadying her.

"Chan and me?"

"It's not my business, so don't feel you have to answer." He escorted her up the steps to the hotel entry. "Will you be all right from here?"

Shoving aside her indignation, Beth reminded herself he didn't know the full extent of her training as a federal agent. She could more than take care of herself.

"I'll be fine. Thank you for escorting me." Beth didn't believe she'd been in any danger, but Chan had a lot on his mind besides their investigation. Too much to worry about her.

Touching the brim of his hat, Caleb smiled. "Anytime, Agent Cartman."

Turning to walk inside, a movement to her left caught her attention. It had been slight, insignificant, if Gabe hadn't been shot and she wasn't already watching for anything unusual.

Sliding her hand into the reticule to grasp her pocket revolver, she walked back down the steps, moving to the corner of the hotel. Whoever she saw had disappeared around the corner toward the back, or maybe dashed across the small distance to the church.

Even as she drew her gun from the reticule, Beth knew it wasn't smart to follow. Still, she moved forward. All she wanted was a glimpse, enough to determine if what she saw was a threat.

The sound of a horse whinnying drew her to the side of the church, then to the back. Holding the gun in front of her, she peered around the corner. Seeing nothing, she let out a shaky breath before turning, and froze.

A man of average height, dressed as a ranch hand with brown hat and boots, blocked her path. A pair of six-shooters strapped around his waist, a feral grin split his plain face.

"Going someplace, girlie?"

Squaring her shoulders, she took a step back, pointing her gun at his chest. "Who are you?"

An amused chuckle blew past his lips a moment before his arm snaked out, gripping her wrist. A second later, he had her back to his chest, her arm twisted behind her. Placing his other arm against her throat, he leaned down to whisper into Beth's ear.

"You know who I am, Agent Cartman." When she tried to break his grip, he tightened his hold, causing her to choke. "I have a message for Marshal Evans."

She winced at the smell of his hot, acrid breath against her neck. "What?"

"You tell him to put his affairs in order. Tell him—" Before he could finish, Beth raised her leg, driving the heel of her boot into his shin.

Cursing, he swung her around, striking her across the face, drawing blood. Dropping her to the ground, he bent down within inches of her face, pressing a gun to her forehead.

"You tell him I'm not leaving town until he's six feet under." Straightening, he kicked her in the side and ran.

By the time Beth regained her breath and rolled onto her knees, Burris was gone. Choking, she touched her face, feeling what she knew to be blood stick to her fingers.

Boots pounded on the ground. "Is that you, Beth?"

Strong arms slipped under hers, helping her to stand. Zeke waited until she gained her balance before dropping his arms. Seeing the blood on her face, he cursed.

"Who did this?"

"Burris."

Swearing again, he wrapped an arm around her waist. "We need to get you to the clinic."

She dug her heels into the ground. "No. Chan doesn't need to see me like this."

"Sorry, but my life won't be worth anything if I *don't* have one of the docs check you out. I'd appreciate it if you wouldn't fight me on this, because then I might have to toss you over my shoulder."

Her face reddened, voice brittle. "You wouldn't."

"Yes, ma'am, I surely would."

Too tired to argue further, she did what Zeke asked, finding no point in making this any worse than it already was going to be. Chan would be furious, and the others wouldn't be any less angry.

Worse, Beth knew her actions were foolish. No matter her talents at handling a gun, she wasn't strong enough to overcome an adversary such as Burris.

It took them several minutes to reach the steps of the clinic. Instead of assisting her up, Zeke swept her into his arms, kicking open the front door.

Dax was the first to respond. "What the hell?"

By then, the others had turned to see who was making such a fuss, Chan rushing toward them. Growling at the sight of Zeke holding Beth against his chest, Chan slipped his arms under her, shifting her to rest against him.

"What happened?"

"Burris."

Whatever Chan was about to say died on his lips when Beth spoke. "Please put me down. It's not as bad as it looks."

Ignoring her, he walked to an empty exam room. "Someone get one of the doctors." Disappearing inside, he laid her on the bed, lighting two of the lanterns just as Clay came into the room.

"Give us some privacy, Chan."

"I'm not leaving her, Doc."

Beth placed a hand on Clay's arm. "It's all right. Please let him stay."

Agreeing, he ran a hand down her legs, arms, and sides, checking for injuries, before focusing on her face. "Did he do this with his hand?"

"Yes. Then kicked me in the side."

"Which side?"

Beth indicated her right. Clay glanced behind him. "You need to turn away while I pull out her blouse to look at her side, Chan."

Not wanting to embarrass Beth, or share the depth of their intimacy, he did as Clay asked. He turned back when the doctor spoke to her again.

"No broken bones, but you will have bruising. There's nothing I can do except offer you laudanum."

"I'd rather have whiskey, Doctor."

Chan chuckled at the expected response. The same as him, she hated using the drug so many had become addicted to.

Several minutes later, Clay had finished suturing the cut on her face and helped her sit up. "You're welcome to stay in here until you're ready to leave. Even if it's tomorrow morning."

"Thank you, but I'd rather return to the hotel and get some rest."

"Only if you have an escort."

"I'll be taking her over, Clay." Chan moved next to the table, putting an arm around her waist to help her stand. "Are you all right, sweetheart?"

Clay didn't miss the endearment, but said nothing. "If you don't need anything, I'm going to relieve Dr. Worthington so he can get some sleep."

"I've got her. Send someone if Gabe wakes up again."

"I will."

Chan bent down, brushing a kiss across her forehead. "Let's get you to the hotel."

Leaving the room, he motioned for Zeke and Mack to come with them. Neither hesitated.

Twenty minutes later, he had her under the covers. Dragging an overstuffed chair to the bed, he reached under the blanket, threading fingers through hers, his other hand stroking her hair.

Her wide, violet eyes searched his. "Please join me, Chan."

A weak smile tilted the corners of his mouth. "I want nothing more, but you need to rest."

"Just to hold me. Nothing more."

Unable to tell her *no*, he stood, stripping to his drawers. Slipping in beside Beth, he tucked an arm under her, resting her against his side.

Resting his chin on the top of her head, he stroked her arm, feeling Beth relax beside him.

Voice thick with exhaustion, she pressed a hand over his chest. "Don't leave me, Chan."

Sucking in a slow breath, he let it out in an even slower whoosh. "I won't leave you, Beth. I'll never leave you."

Chapter Twenty-Two

Short, slender fingers worked quickly to count bundles of bills, stacking them at the end of the table. He repeated the process thirty times before wrapping each bundle with string and setting them aside.

This continued for another hour before he counted out a specific number of bound notes, topping them with a row of Chinese language books before wrapping them in paper for delivery to the post office. In a few days, he'd package more bundles, again placing a layer of books on top.

It had been the same for almost a year, becoming easier with each package mailed. They'd been paid well for printing, packaging, and mailing the fake notes. So well, they were considering buying one of the new buildings at the end of town.

There was enough room to move the printing business into half of the downstairs, rent the other half, and live on the second floor. They'd have twice the living space of their present apartment, enough for four bedrooms, living room, kitchen, and small dining room. It would be as if they lived in a palace.

Nodding to the man standing several feet away, he handed him the package, already addressed and ready to mail.

Chan had let Beth sleep, not waking her when May delivered a tray of coffee and sweet breads for when she woke. During this time, Chan made a quick trip to the clinic to check on Gabe, who hadn't woken that morning. Returning to the room, he wrote down what they'd learned, which wasn't much, and what still needed to be done. The list was short.

They'd yet to send a telegram to Thad, which bought them time to continue the investigation. Gave Chan more time to convince Beth to stay, give their fledgling relationship a chance.

His determination to shield his heart hadn't worked for long. Chan conceded it had been a losing battle from the moment he'd entered the Big Pine jail to see her sitting across the desk from Sterling.

She'd been as beautiful as he remembered. So much so, his heart had stuttered, breath hitching under the weight of old feelings. Chan had done all he could to ignore the craving for his former lover. His resolve had chipped away little by little each day until he'd given up.

This time, though, Beth seemed to be right with him. Chan was far from ready to believe he'd won her over, but hoped the ending would be much different than the last time.

A knock had him setting the paper and pencil aside. Opening the door, he stepped into the hall next to Mack.

"Is it Gabe?"

"He's awake and doing better."

"So this visit isn't about my brother."

Mack shook his head. "Enoch saw Burris this morning in McCall's."

"What?" Chan couldn't hide his incredulity.

"Eating breakfast as if he hadn't shot our sheriff last night. The man either has incredible nerve or is a complete fool. Enoch waited until he was finished and followed him to Chinatown, then went to the jail. Beau and Cash went with him to Chinatown, checked every shop, but Burris had vanished."

"He's taunting us. Letting me know he can get to me anytime and anywhere."

"We won't let that happen, Chan."

"I appreciate it, but all he needs is one clean shot."

Mack clasped a hand on his shoulder. "Then we won't let him get it. Hex, Zeke, Dutch, Caleb, and Mack have joined Beau and Cash. Noah, Nick, and several of the Pelletier men are searching the town and guarding the trails in and out. Dom Lucero and Curly even rode in to help out. It's a matter of time before Burris is located and arrested."

Threading fingers through his hair, Chan hooked his thumbs into the waistband of his pants. "I don't want anyone to get hurt because of me."

"It's not your choice. Burris shot and almost killed Gabe. You know Caleb and I served under him during the war."

"I remember hearing that. You and Caleb were majors under Gabe."

"Right. He's my boss, former commander, and a good friend. We're going after Burris whether you want us to or not."

Chastised, Chan looked away. Gabe's deputies weren't just employees. They were his closest friends, people he'd always be able to count on.

"Do you have any idea where he might be hiding out?"

"None. The same as with Gabe and Beth, he strikes and runs. The man's a real coward and doesn't fight fair. If we don't catch him, he's going to wait until you're alone and shoot you square in the back. It would be best if you stayed out of sight until we find him."

"I refuse to hide, Mack."

"It would be the smart move, Chan. Keep watch on Beth, make sure she's safe and recovers."

"I'm taking her out to the Pelletier ranch. Dax told me she can stay as long as needed."

Mack quirked a brow. "Did she agree to this?"

Chan's mouth twisted into a grimace. "I haven't had a chance to tell her."

Crossing his arms, Mack shook his head, chuckling. "Good luck. Beth doesn't seem to be the kind of woman who takes orders well."

"Appears to be a condition of the women who move to Splendor."

"Obstinate, stubborn, independent?" Mack's lips twitched.

Chan choked out a laugh. "All three."

Gyp slid from his horse, tired, thirsty, and ready for a real bed. First, he had to go by the telegraph office. If no message from Simon awaited him, the plan would stay the same. He and his two new associates would ride to Splendor and complete the assignment. If a telegram was there, it meant the orders had changed.

Leaving the two men behind, he stomped his boots on the boardwalk, cautiously glancing around. Gyp believed nobody would recognize him from his part in freeing Simon Priest from jail. Still, he'd always been a careful man, refusing to take chances.

Straightening, he made a slow, vigilant turn. He saw no sign of the sheriff or any of his deputies. Satisfied, he closed the short distance to the telegraph office, relieved to find no messages from Simon.

The relief didn't last long. His mind turned to the job in Splendor. He'd been working for Simon and his brother, Damien, for a while. Moving one of the printing operations from a bigger city back east to the small town in Montana never made sense to him. They'd had a good system going with excellent distribution.

Neither of the Priest brothers had explained, not even when he asked. Over time, Gyp discovered they relocated because one of their coney dealers was being questioned by the Secret Service.

Almost overnight, the Priests had closed down, moving everything to Splendor. The brothers had considered the growing frontier town for some time, had prepared themselves, including having Simon travel west to confirm a new association with a new partner.

The move had been a success. Simon's arrest had changed little, except he could no longer show his face in Moosejaw, Big Pine, or Splendor. The job of making occasional visits to their partners in Montana shifted to Gyp. More responsibility and better pay suited him fine. He'd do whatever they wanted as long as more money came with it.

Crossing the street, he headed straight into the closest saloon. They wouldn't be staying in Big Pine more than one night, and he meant to make the most of it. The trail to Splendor would take at least five hours, more if they had to fight through one of Montana's frequent storms or came across the renegade band of Crow. He'd worry about all that tomorrow.

Today, he'd spend hours playing cards, drinking whiskey, and not worrying about the future.

Splendor

Beth's eyes opened to slits, her mind straining to remember why her head pounded and side throbbed.

Rubbing her temples, the events of the night before came rushing back.

Burris. His threat to Chan. The chilling, soulless gleam in his eyes.

The recollection produced a cold ball of dread to form in her stomach. She had no doubt Burris would do all he could to fulfill his promise of putting Chan six feet under. And she had yet to tell Chan of the threat.

Groaning, she leveraged herself up to sit on the side of the bed. Beth knew he'd stayed with her most of the night. Glancing around, there was no sign Chan had even been there. Her disappointment was acute. He'd done what he promised, then left.

Making quick work of her morning ablutions, she took a good look at her face for the first time since the attack. The sutures were small, but there'd still be a scar, even if slight. The bruising looked worse than it felt. From experience, it would continue to worsen before the colors began to fade. At least she saw no sign of swelling.

Retrieving her reticule, she confirmed the pocket pistol still lay inside. For a moment, Beth considered strapping her dual six-shooters around her waist, discarding the idea as fast as the thought came. The guns would do nothing except draw unwanted attention, which she didn't need.

She had to focus on finishing the investigation and making a recommendation to Thad. With what she and Chan had already learned, Beth didn't see a reason to stay in Splendor any longer.

They'd made a mistake believing the forgers would print and distribute fake notes from a remote town in the middle of nowhere. The stagecoach came through on a regular basis, but it was several days' ride to a railroad.

Either passengers carried packages of bills with them on the stage or those involved used the mail, which meant the counterfeit notes still traveled by stagecoach. She'd thought of this before. This time, the possibilities carried more of an impact.

Move the bills inside luggage, or post the package with Bernie Griggs. Either way, the imitations traveled by stage. It didn't matter where they were printed as much as how they were distributed.

"Of course," Beth whispered.

Grabbing the brown suede hat she often used when away from home, she hurried down the stairs and to the street. Beth needed to find Chan, tell him about the threat from Burris and explain her thoughts on the investigation.

They didn't need to waste any more time interviewing or searching for a hidden printing press. All their attention should now focus on mail received by Bernie and the baggage of departing passengers.

Chapter Twenty-Three

Beth searched the town for Chan, not finding him in the jail or anywhere else. In fact, she found just one deputy. Dutch McFarlin had made a turn of the main street, approaching with a worried expression.

"I'm looking for Chan."

His features softened as he nodded to the street behind them. "They're all at the clinic."

"All?"

A low chuckle blew through his lips. "Darndest thing. Seems Lena and Suzanne decided to have their babies today."

"Oh my." Turning, she picked up her skirts and ran to the clinic.

Starting up the steps, she stopped when the door opened. Zeke and Hex walked out, a smile on each face.

"How are they?"

"According to Worthington and McCord, Lena and Suzanne are doing fine." Zeke rubbed his jaw, glancing over his shoulder. "It's a little too, well...much for us bachelors."

"Then I'll take your places." She passed them on the steps, then stopped. "How's Gabe?"

Hex's features sobered, the smile gone. "He had a bad night, woke up with a fever. They're trying to bring it down while tending to the ladies. Beau rode out to get Rachel and Rosemary."

Beth had heard Rachel Pelletier had been a Union nurse during the war, and Rosemary Masters had trained under her. Both put in time as often as they could at the clinic.

"Usually Suzanne and Lena would be helping with the births," Zeke said.

"I'll see if there's anything I can do." Shoving open the door, Beth took a cautious step inside, taking in the scene.

Nick paced the full length of the room, stopping at the bottom of the stairs to the second floor each time. Walter did the same, wiping sweat from his brow. Each muttered as they walked, shoved hands into their pockets, then pulled them out to swing by their sides.

Ruth Paige, the reverend's wife, Olivia, and Sylvia Mackey sat together along one wall while the other deputies spoke among themselves. After a few more minutes, Mack Mackey kissed his wife on the cheek before leaving with Caleb and Cash.

Chan leaned against a wall near the stairs, arms crossed. From her position, it appeared his eyes were closed. She wondered if he'd gotten any sleep the night before.

Head lifting, the hint of a smile brightened his face for a split second before the somber expression returned. He looked exhausted, as he should be after all that had happened.

Walking to him, she placed a hand on his arm. "How are you doing?"

Covering her hand with his, Chan studied the bruising and sutures on her face. "I'm fine. Surprised to see you here. How are you feeling?" Lifting a hand, he stroked her cheek with a light, barely noticeable touch.

Closing her eyes, she allowed herself a moment before letting go of his arm and moving away. "I'm fine. My side is sore."

"You're lucky he didn't crack or break a rib," he ground out, unable to conceal his anger at Burris. "We are going to find him, Beth."

Pursing her lips, she lowered her voice, leaning toward him. "Do you have a few minutes to speak with me?"

"We *are* talking."

"Not here, Chan. Someplace more private."

Curiosity had him grasping her elbow. "Lena and Suzanne are in rooms upstairs. We can use the exam room over there."

He guided her past the others, ignoring their inquisitive stares. Closing the door behind them, he walked to the window, drawing the curtains closed.

Crossing his arms, he leaned against the table, his gaze narrowing on Beth. "All right. We're alone."

His wary expression, lips pressed into a thin line, had her pausing for a moment before starting.

"Besides someone riding out with fake notes in their saddlebags, there are only two ways to move the money out of Splendor. They are either sent through the mail, which travels with the stage, or passengers hide the notes in their luggage.”

A deep line appeared between his brows. “And?”

“If the counterfeiters are here, we should concentrate on how the money gets out of Splendor.”

“How do you propose we do that? Search every passenger? Bernie can’t be expected to question every person who posts mail.”

“And we aren’t allowed to check packages without a good reason.”

“Right.” Chan paced across the room, stopping to whirl around to look at her. “Judge Collins.”

She took a couple steps toward him, head tilted to one side. “What about him?”

“He’s aware of our investigation. I can request an order allowing us to inspect packages.”

“Do you think he’ll do it?”

“It’s a case his friend, President Grant, wants solved. So yes, he’ll issue the order.”

Nodding in understanding, she wrapped her arms around her waist.

“What is it, Beth?”

“There’s something else.”

Closing the distance between them, he settled his hands on her shoulders. “Tell me.” Gently moving his hands up and down her arms, Chan waited.

“Burris gave me a message for you.”

“Which was?”

Licking her lips, her worried expression gave it all away. "He's going to put you six feet under."

Guilt ate at Beth. She'd delivered the two important messages, leaving something out. Thad had ordered her not to divulge the additional information to Chan, arguing the marshal didn't need to know what they'd suspected for a long time.

The longer Beth worked with Chan, the more she realized the fallacy of Thad's thinking. Withholding any of their suspicions didn't help the investigation.

She and Chan had left the room to face a tense group of people, their attention focused on the stairs. Minutes later, they heard it. Or them.

The cries of newborns filtered down the stairs. Nick tried to push past Beau, who'd returned with Rachel and Rosemary while Beth and Chan had been talking. The deputy held up his hands, refusing to let Nick pass before the doctors let them know it was all right.

For a moment, Beth thought Chan would have to help Beau hold back a distressed Nick. But the new father backed away, taking in a deep breath. His hands shook when he lifted them to thread fingers through his hair.

The patch over one eye, his dark hair, and olive complexion gave him the look of a pirate. Rugged, handsome, and devoted to his wife, Beth could understand how Suzanne had fallen in love with Nick.

Several minutes ticked by before an exhausted Doc Worthington came downstairs, his gaze locking on Nick. "Suzanne is doing fine. As is your son."

"A boy?"

A small smile turned up the corners of the doctor's mouth. "If you're ready, you can go upstairs and meet him."

By now, Olivia had moved beside her father to grip his hand. "Can we both go up?"

"Now's as good a time as any to meet your brother. Neither of you will be able to stay more than a few minutes. Suzanne needs to rest." Worthington opened the door to where Gabe slept, stopping at Chan's question.

"What about Lena?"

The doctor motioned for Chan to follow, then did the same to Walter and Nora. "I'm going to tell Gabe now."

Crowding around the bed, the four stared at the motionless figure. His face hadn't regained its color, his lips slightly blue. Worthington grabbed another blanket, placing it on top of the one already covering Gabe.

Walter moved next to the bed, setting a hand on his son's arm. "Gabe?" When he didn't answer, Walter spoke his name again. This time, Gabe stirred.

Eyes opening to unfocused slits, he blinked and tried to sit up. Walter and Doc Worthington gently kept him in place.

Opening his mouth, Gabe coughed. "Water."

Taking a sip from the glass his father held, Gabe's gaze moved to Worthington. "Where's Lena?"

Features softening, the doctor smiled. "Lena is upstairs with your daughter."

"Daughter?"

"That's right."

A new resolve flashed across Gabe's face. "How is she?"

"Tired, but good."

"I want to see her." Gabe tried to sit up again, wincing in pain before falling back.

"You'll see her and your daughter, but it will take a little more time."

"Time?" Gabe croaked out the word, his throat thick. His eyes closed before opening again. "I need to see them."

Walter shot a glance at Chan, then Nora. "Stubborn as ever. Can he be moved, Doctor?"

"It would be too risky. However, I can have Rachel bring down his daughter. When Lena feels up to it, we'll help get her down here, too."

"I'll follow you upstairs, Doctor." Nora left the room with Worthington, barely containing her excitement at seeing her niece.

"We'll have to ask Rachel if it's too early to move the baby."

"But you're the doctor," Nora said as they reached the second floor.

His lips tilted into a grin. "Yes, but my niece is the boss."

Burris watched the comings and goings at the clinic from an unused room upstairs at Ruby's Grand Palace, never finding a good opportunity to get the man he wanted alone. In fact, he hadn't seen Chan Evans at all. Burris estimated it wouldn't be long before Ruby, the owner of the Palace, made her rounds. He might be able to avoid her for a while, but not long, and he couldn't take the chance of getting caught.

Burris had thought the number of people keeping watch on the sheriff would've dwindled by now. Instead, he'd noticed an increase in the number of visitors. It seemed odd to have so many people sitting around, waiting for Gabe Evans to recover.

Standing, he stretched, bending from one side to the other while still keeping watch out the window. Burris stilled at a noise in the hall. Moving slowly toward another door, he slipped into a room used for storage.

Chairs were stacked four high, two wardrobes covered in dust were placed against one wall while several small tables took up the rest of the space. He moved farther into the room, squeezing behind one of the wardrobes a moment before the door opened.

Ruby placed her hands on ample hips, looking around. Her gaze settled on one of the wardrobes. "There you are."

Burris held his breath as her footsteps came closer, his hand moving to the butt of his gun. He stiffened at the sound of unoiled hinges creaking as a wardrobe door opened. The same wardrobe he hid behind.

Depending on the timing and necessity, the outlaw had no issue with killing a woman. He might cringe at cutting down a proper lady, but status wouldn't stop him. Murdering a madam in her place of business wouldn't cause him a whisper of guilt.

The hesitancy came from being discovered by those responding to a gunshot. Hearing Ruby rummage through the contents of the wardrobe, Burris considered other ways of silencing her. Strangulation would be quiet, if he kept her from kicking and scratching him. A blow to the head would work well. Quick and efficient, as long as he buried the butt of his gun in the right spot.

"Where is it?"

Burris tensed further at Ruby's muttering. He wanted her to find whatever she was looking for and leave.

Closing the door, she opened another, continuing to sort through whatever was inside. Burris had reached the point where he'd decided to stop the search himself when she muttered again.

"I knew you were in here." The rustling of fabric confirmed she'd found what she sought.

Heavy footsteps on the wood floor signaled her leaving. Burris let out a breath, moved his hand off the butt of his gun, then jumped.

A burst of gunfire, then a shrill scream flooded through the upstairs window from the street below.

Chapter Twenty-Four

Slipping from his hiding place behind the wardrobe, Burris peeked out the window, spotting three deputies running toward the front of the Grand Palace. Shouts and panicked voices came from several others who remained out of his sight.

It didn't take long before Burris saw the reason for the screams. Two of the deputies carried a body down the street to the undertaker's office. With the continuing confusion, Burris made a quick decision to slip out of the Palace before anyone noticed him.

He knew Evans wouldn't stay away from the clinic where his brother recovered. All he had to do was keep watch for the marshal to appear late in the evening, come up behind him, and end this. Evans wouldn't know his life was over until he hit the ground.

Chan scrubbed both hands up and down his face. He hadn't left the clinic for more than a few minutes and it was now past sunset. Beth had fetched food for everyone, ran errands, and at one point, sent a telegram to Thad.

It was beyond time they provided the senior agent with an update, even if nothing had been discovered. At least they had a plan for going forward, a way to discover if fake notes were being sent from Splendor. If they were, it wouldn't take long to scour the town and find the source.

As far as anyone knew, the only two printing presses were located in the Chinese bookstore and the office of the Splendor Herald. A search of each had provided no answers. Unless a third press operated somewhere in town, they'd missed something.

A light touch on Chan's arm drew his attention to Beth. He followed her gaze to the stairs and stood. A tired but determined looking Lena came down, Rachel behind her holding the infant girl.

Earlier, Gabe hadn't woken to meet his daughter. This time, Lena informed the doctors she wouldn't be leaving his room until he got to see the tiny bundle.

Chan opened the door to the room where his brother still healed, holding it open for Lena and Rachel. Before following them inside, he motioned for Beth to join them. When she hesitated, he shot her an encouraging smile, motioning again. A flood of warmth washed through her at the invitation. The gesture may have meant little to him, but she saw it as much more.

Stepping past him, Beth took a position against a wall away from the bed. She felt out of place, a stranger among people who knew each other well. When no one said anything about her inclusion, Beth relaxed, curiosity winning out over any sense of discomfort.

She'd seen many babies, held a handful, but never a newborn. The wrinkled face fascinated her, as did the tiny hands and fingers, the small thatch of dark hair.

Lena's fingers stroked down Gabe's face before she leaned forward, whispering into his ear. Beth watched as his eyelids opened to slits, then widened when he recognized the woman next to him.

"Lena." He croaked her name, throat dry, lips parched. "Water."

Taking a glass from Chan's hand, she held it to her husband's lips. "Only a sip."

Swallowing a small amount, the corners of his mouth twitched. "I'd prefer whiskey."

"I'm certain you would." Lena lowered the glass, handing it back to Chan.

The whimpering of a baby drew Gabe's attention. Eyes wide, his breath hitched at the sight of his daughter in Rachel's arms. When she slid the infant into Lena's, he tried to sit up, sending an evil glare at Chan when he gently pushed him back down.

"Gabe, meet your daughter." Lena leaned closer so he could get a better look. "She has your eyes."

Pulling his arm from under the covers, he reached out before snatching his hand back.

"You aren't going to hurt her, Gabe."

"I don't think I'm ready to hold her yet." An odd expression crossed his face when he looked at Lena. "What's her name?"

"I decided to wait until we could pick out a name together."

The deep lines etched on his face softened. Opening his mouth to speak, she smiled, placing a finger across his lips.

"We'll wait until you're back home." Leaning down, she kissed Gabe, then held their daughter in front of him again.

"She's so beautiful, Lena." His voice grew stronger each minute, his eyes watering as he stared at the infant. "Have Suzanne and Nick had a chance to see her?" He touched the top of her head, stroking the silken hair.

"That's right. You don't know." Lena glanced at Chan, who stepped closer.

His voice lowered to a reverent tone. "Suzanne had a baby boy within minutes of your daughter being born. Poor kid looks a lot like Nick." Chan chuckled as a grin tipped the corners of his brother's mouth.

Several feet away, Beth watched, tears welling in her eyes. At one time, she'd been close to her parents, sharing every part of her life with them. Although not estranged, it had been a long time since she'd felt the level of connection she witnessed between Lena, Gabe, and Chan. If Walter, Nora, and her husband, Wyatt, had been present, it would be more of the same.

Once again, Beth saw herself as an outsider, an unexpected visitor watching an intensely personal moment. If she hadn't walked out on Chan two years before, she might be the one holding a baby, discussing names, feeling loved.

After what she'd done, Beth knew her chance of belonging to such a family had been lost. At least with Chan.

"What do you think?"

Startled at Chan's voice, she straightened. Beth hadn't heard him approach. She felt his comforting hand on her shoulder.

"I think she's the most precious thing I've ever seen."

Chan ignored the moisture in her eyes, knowing she wouldn't appreciate his comfort in front of the family. As much as he wanted her to stay, do all he could to convince her Splendor could be her home, the odds were Beth would board the stage once the investigation was over. Unless he could come up with a good reason for her to stay.

"I'm ready to get some fresh air. Would you like to come with me, Agent Cartman?"

A small smile curved her lips. "Yes, I would, Marshal Evans."

Gyp rode ahead of his two partners, clearing his head from an evening consuming a bottle of whiskey by their campfire a few miles outside of Splendor.

He'd ridden into town earlier in the day, watching as a drunken cowboy shot another outside a place called the Grand Palace. Waiting until the crowd dispersed, Gyp had stopped for a couple drinks, eaten, then taken an indirect route to their primary source, making certain no one followed. Slipping inside, his eyes had shown amusement at the stunned faces.

They'd expected Simon Priest, not a hardened gunslinger who knew a great deal about the operation. Not that he cared. He'd been given the job of assuring his boss their printers were producing and mailing the number of notes in the agreement. Most important, Priest required confirmation no one had been snooping around, asking questions.

Less than an hour later, satisfied with what he'd learned, Gyp left with two small packages tucked under an arm. One he posted with Bernie Griggs. The other he slid into his saddlebag, glancing around to make certain no one watched.

Gyp keeping a batch of fake notes hadn't been part of his agreement with Simon. After thinking about it all the way from Cheyenne, he'd decided to make his move.

He wanted out. The idea had been forming for a long time, since well before freeing Simon from the Big Pine jail.

Most of his share of the money had been stashed in two banks in different states. The rest he kept with him, hidden among his meager belongings. No one would think a gunman who lost at cards and drank too much would have a large amount of money with him.

He'd stay a couple nights in Splendor before rejoining his two *partners*. They'd follow the stage to Big Pine, stopping it before it reached Moosejaw. It seemed an odd plan. The usual plan called for the packages to reach their final destination. Rarely was he asked to deviate.

Taking a seat inside the Dixie, Gyp ordered a drink, waving away a barmaid who offered him company. He needed to think, figure out why the order to rob the stage bothered him so much.

Simon and his brother, Damien, spent days planning every move before sending orders to those who worked with them. Gyp liked to believe he'd been one of their most loyal associates. Yet their latest order bothered him, warning bells sounding in his head.

The two men were extremely smart, their sole purpose of counterfeiting to revive the Southern cause. Gyp understood. He, too, served the South, felt the frustration and anger when Lee surrendered to Grant.

Unlike the Priests, he'd changed professions from being a soldier to a gun for hire. Gyp also didn't see an opportunity for the South to overthrow Grant's Union. It had been several years since the surrender at Appomattox. In his mind, any chance at retaking the country wouldn't happen in his lifetime and probably not the next, if ever.

Resting his head in his hands, Gyp stared into his second shot of whiskey. Running through every situation he could think of, he lifted his head, making a decision.

They'd follow the stage through Big Pine and into Moosejaw. At that point, Gyp would either steal the mailbag or let the stage ride out. If the second turned out to be his decision, he'd pay the two others from his own funds, leaving them and the Priest brothers behind.

Chan and Beth, exhausted and hungry, walked up the steps of the Eagle's Nest. They'd have supper while discussing their meeting with Bernie Griggs.

The postmaster had surprised them by being more cooperative than expected when they requested he watch for packages suspected of holding bogus money.

Ordering, Chan leaned toward her, reaching under the table to take her hand in his. "I need to ride out to the Lucero ranch in the morning. Would you like to come with me?"

The way her eyes widened indicated how much he'd surprised Beth. "If you don't think the Luceros will mind."

"They welcome everyone." Picking up his glass of wine, he took a sip, not wanting to scare her off while needing to understand his reasons. "I'd also like them to meet you."

Amusement crinkled the corners of his eyes at her startled expression. His fingers squeezed hers before he released his grip.

Heart pounding, she tried not to believe his invitation meant anything. "Why would they want to meet me?"

Waiting until the server set their meals on the table, he picked up his fork. "The same reason as Lena and Gabe. You're important to me, Beth." Before he could say more than he wanted to reveal, Chan placed a bite of roast into his mouth.

Unable to stop staring, she bit her lower lip, fingers tightening on the stem of her glass. He'd already admitted to still loving her, and he knew she loved him.

"You're important to me, too, Chan."

Straightening, his brown eyes darkened to pools of deep umber, the same color as when he made love. A shiver ran through her, hunger disappearing as their gazes locked and held.

He was more than just important to her. Beth loved him. If only she could say the words.

Chapter Twenty-Five

Beth heard the soft knock on her door, already knowing who stood in the hall. She took another look in the mirror before standing.

Morning had come early after a long evening of drinking coffee, eating pie, and talking. Chan had been a complete gentleman, walking her upstairs, brushing a kiss across her lips, but not asking to enter her room. She knew he was trying to spare her reputation. Still, the disappointment stung, especially since he'd already spent the night in her hotel room.

As a widow, the standards of propriety were not as strict, allowing her more freedom without the need of a chaperone. Although they'd been discreet in Austin, Beth was certain a number of people knew about their liaisons. She also believed the same was true in Splendor.

Opening the door, she smiled at the sight of Chan. Before she knew what he planned, Beth was pushed back inside, the door closing as he backed her up against it. His mouth crushed against hers, hands moving up and down her back.

Aligning their bodies, he deepened the kiss. Long moments later, he pulled away, resting his forehead against hers.

Voice thick and ragged, he moved his lips to her ear. "I shouldn't have left last night."

Breath coming in short gasps, she gripped his shoulders. "Oh?"

"I didn't sleep at all."

"No?" She whispered the question against his neck.

"I spent the entire night thinking about you." Cupping her face in both hands, he kissed her again before taking a step away. "We need to get out of here before we end up in bed." Leaning forward, he kissed her again. "I'd like to take you to breakfast."

"That would be wonderful, Chan."

Taking her hand, he led Beth into the hall. "Afterward, we need to visit Bernie again to see if he's come across anything interesting."

She'd supported convincing the postmaster to closely scrutinize packages, paying attention to those who showed only Splendor in the left corner. What bothered Beth was Bernie himself. Although promising to do what he could, he wasn't comfortable asking questions about a package's contents.

Shy and fidgety, he didn't like confrontations, preferring to please everyone. The more she'd thought about it, the less Beth believed Bernie would be as helpful as she'd first thought.

Seated at the table in the dining room, her gaze kept wandering outside. Cullen Burris's threat weighed on her. The gunman meant what he'd said about killing Chan.

"Are you going to share your thoughts?"

Chan's voice drew her attention away from the view outside. Worrying her bottom lip, she fingered the napkin in her lap. "I'm concerned about you."

His mouth twisted into a smug grin. "Me?

"Burris is serious about killing you, yet you don't appear troubled."

Chan's grin slipped, the humor fading from his face. Moving his chair toward hers, he settled a hand over hers. "Burris is a coward. He'll come after me at night from behind. He knows facing off with me would be a death sentence."

Turning her hand over, she threaded her fingers through his. "You're that much better than him?"

The smug expression returned. "Yes, I am. The difference is the man doesn't play fair. But he's also patient. He'll wait until night when I'm alone."

"Then you shouldn't be out at night."

"That isn't going to happen, Beth."

"But—"

He silenced her with a finger over her lips. "Gabe's deputies know all about him and the threat. They'll look out for Burris and cover me after dark."

Chan had no plans to tell Beth about what he, Caleb, Mack, Beau, and the other deputies had discussed. He wanted the threat of Burris gone. Wanted Beth safe.

As soon as Gabe was recovered enough to return home with Lena and their baby, Chan would become the bait to draw Burris out. The outlaw would be arrested, stand trial, and if all went as expected, hang for murder.

"I'll be with you at night."

A brow lifted, lips twitching in amusement. "Is that so, Agent Cartman?"

Face turning red, she huffed out a sigh. "You know what I mean, Chan. If you need to be out at night, I'll go with you."

"No." He squeezed her hand, then pulled free to grab his cup of coffee.

"No?"

"I won't allow you to be a possible target for Burris."

Crossing her arms, Beth's lips pressed together in a disgruntled line. "Let me remind you that I'm capable of taking care of myself. I'm also not a woman you can order around."

Growing quiet while the server set down their food, she picked up a fork, stabbing a piece of ham. Chan watched as she chewed furiously, swallowed, then stabbed another piece. If she weren't so angry, it would be amusing.

"I'm not trying to control you, Beth. I just need to know you're safe."

His words, the sincerity in his voice, had her softening. But only a little. Beth refused to have him think of her as needing his protection when she'd been taking care of herself for a long time.

"We need to talk about Bernie."

The change of topics had him narrowing his gaze. "What about Bernie?"

"We aren't going to get what we need from him, Chan."

"Why is that?"

"Bernie's too nice a man to question people about their packages. The best we can hope for is he'll let us know who sends out packages with just the town shown as the sender." She fingered her coffee cup, staring into the cooling liquid. "Truthfully, I don't believe Thad was right about the notes originating in Splendor."

Setting down his fork and knife, he leaned back in his chair. He knew what was coming, but still wasn't prepared. "You've decided to leave." *Again*, he thought, but held it inside.

The small lump in her throat grew until she couldn't swallow. Beth didn't want to leave, but unless Chan asked her to stay, she'd be on a stage within the week. Thad would insist on it, and she'd have no excuse to remain any longer.

"If the notes aren't being printed in Splendor, then there's no reason for me to stay. Is there?" She lifted her gaze to meet his before Chan looked past her to the street outside.

"Stay here." He stood, his hand already on the butt of his six-shooter. Hearing her chair scrape across the wood floor, he glared at her, voice hard as stone before opening the door. "Do *not* follow me, Beth."

Standing, she rushed to follow. "I won't be left behind."

Whirling around, Chan grabbed her arm, shoving her against the outside wall of the St. James Hotel. "I think Burris just walked into McCall's."

"I'm going with you," she hissed, trying to shove him away.

Cursing under his breath, Chan glanced over his shoulder at the restaurant across the street. "It might not be him."

"In that case, I'm in no danger."

Shaking his head, Chan released her. "Stay behind me and do what I say. Do you understand, Beth?"

"Fine. Now, let's hurry before he slips out the back." Ignoring his orders, she pushed past him, dodging wagons and riders as she crossed the street.

"Dammit, Beth." Running, he caught up to her as her hand gripped the door's handle.

Pulling her hand away, he tugged her behind him. "I'll go inside first."

Not responding, she pursed her lips. Slipping a hand into a pocket, she gripped the handle of her pocket pistol and glanced around.

Chan did the same as he walked toward the owner. Betts and her husband had owned McCall's long enough to differentiate between locals and those passing through.

"Morning, Marshal. Are you here for a late breakfast or early lunch?" Betts's broad smile was warm.

"I'm looking for a man who came in a few minutes ago. Several inches taller than me, brown hat and boots."

Betts shook her head as she looked around. "Don't see anyone like that in here. He might have come in while I was in the kitchen."

"He didn't come out the front."

She motioned for Chan and Beth to follow her down a short hall to the back door. "He would've had to go out this way." Betts shoved the door open, all three looking outside.

Moving past her, Chan stepped to the ground, looking up and down the street. He saw no sign of Burris.

"I *know* he came into the restaurant."

Beth searched the street, her gaze lingering on the clinic before settling on Ruby's Palace. "We need to look in there." She started crossing the street before Chan realized her destination.

Catching up, he took one side of the Palace while Beth ran around the other, meeting in back.

"Nothing," Chan said.

"Maybe he's inside."

"He may not have come this way at all, Beth."

"Are you certain you saw Burris?"

Chan nodded. "He was across the street from the Eagle's Nest, watching us. When he saw I'd spotted him, he disappeared into McCall's."

"Then he either had a horse hidden somewhere or has to be nearby. Come on." Without waiting for him, Beth ran back to the front and through the door.

The inside was dark with few lanterns to guide them through the cavernous space. Skirting around tables and chairs, they headed toward the stairs, ignoring the area behind the stage. That was when they heard the scream.

Chan moved past her, taking the stairs two at a time, holding his gun before him. Another scream stalled his progress. Loud and shrill, as if in fear for her life.

He walked in the direction of a second woman's angry voice, keeping his back against the common wall of the upstairs bedrooms. Chan recognized it as Ruby Walsh. He assumed the screams came from one of her ladies.

Inching closer, he shot a look at Beth, who'd taken a position on an opposite wall. Her gun was trained on the rooms between her and Chan.

At his nod, she edged closer, stopping when he held up his hand. Ruby shouted, her voice rising above a third scream.

Chan hurried forward, motioning Beth to stay in place. Gripping the knob, he prepared to open the door when a bullet ripped through the thin veneer, passing within inches of him.

"The next bullet will be aimed at your head."

Cullen Burris.

Before he could react, another gunshot split the silence. This time, it was followed by another scream, a thud, and deep, stomach-clenching groan.

Chapter Twenty-Six

Gyp walked up to the counter in the telegraph office, waiting while Bernie assisted another customer. If all went as planned, he expected a telegram from Simon to be waiting.

Stiffening at what sounded like a gunshot, he looked out the window, finding nothing amiss. No one on the boardwalk reacted as if they'd heard it, too. Shrugging, he pulled a cigar from a pocket and returned to the counter. Before he had a chance to light it, Bernie looked at him.

"May I help you?"

"Is there a telegram waiting for Tom Smith?"

Bernie pulled a box from under the counter, rifling through the messages before lifting one out. "Here it is. Came from Kansas City." He handed it to Gyp.

Not reacting, he pulled a coin from a pocket, setting it on the counter. "Thanks."

Gyp didn't open it right away, preferring to be alone when reading the contents. Stepping onto the boardwalk, his body went rigid at the unmistakable pop of another gunshot. This time, several people looked around while others backed up against the buildings.

Gyp ran in the direction of the gunfire, drawing his six-shooter as he darted around people too panicked to move. When another shot rang out on the street, he picked up his pace.

He didn't know why he cared about what was happening. The town had deputies to take care of whatever was going on. Instead of backing away, his legs continued to pump. Gyp halted outside Ruby's Palace, then ducked at the sound of breaking glass from above.

Covering his head, he crouched low, moving as close to the front of the building as possible. The hoarse scream of a man's voice drew closer. A second later, a body landed on the ground not far from him.

Instead of finding the dead body he expected, the man rose, pointing his gun at Gyp. On instinct, he raised his own weapon, aimed, and fired. The first bullet hit the man in his chest. The second pierced his stomach.

Stumbling backward, his mouth opened, but no words came out before he crumbled to the ground, expelling his last breath.

Staggering to his knees, then standing, Gyp stared down at the dead man. He didn't recognize him. Sliding the gun into its holster, he backed away, stopping at a shout from someone emerging from Ruby's.

"Hold up!"

Gyp's eyes widened at the sight of a badge on the man's shirt. "What can I do for you, Marshal?"

"Are you the man who shot him?"

His chiseled jaw tightened, eyes boring into Chan's. "I am. He fell to the ground, stood, and pointed his gun at me. I shot first."

Chan studied the man's face, wondering if he'd known Burris. "What's your name?"

"Tom Smith. I'm just passing through."

"Where you from?"

"No place in particular."

Though he didn't remember ever meeting Smith before, Chan felt an intense stab of unease. "How long will you be in Splendor?"

Shrugging, Gyp took a step away. "Another day. Maybe two."

"You need to stay long enough to explain what happened to Sheriff Evans."

"I'll go to the jail now." Gyp turned away. He had no intention of speaking with the sheriff, his deputies, or anyone else. The man drew on him, he defended himself. There wasn't more he could tell the sheriff.

"He isn't there."

"Then I'll speak with a deputy." A lie, but the marshal didn't know that.

Beth joined Chan next to the body. "Is it Burris?"

Chan nodded. "I need to let the undertaker know."

She shot a look at the man on the other side of Burris. "I'm Federal Agent Elizabeth Cartman. Are you the one who shot him?"

Gyp nodded, unwilling to explain a second time.

"His name is Tom Smith. Says Burris drew on him first."

"I thought the fall would've killed him," Beth said, looking between the body and Smith.

"If there's nothing else, I'll go speak with one of the deputies."

They watched him leave.

"He won't go to the jail," Chan said.

Beth shook her head. "No, he won't."

"How are Ruby and her girl?" Chan asked.

"Ruby's taking care of her. She's an amazing woman. Unafraid, but angry at Burris. If Smith hadn't shot him, I'm certain Ruby would've."

Neither had noticed the crowd of people surrounding them or Caleb and Mack staring at the body. Chan took a few minutes to talk to the deputies, explaining about the drama inside the Palace, how Burris had jumped from a window, and Tom Smith shooting him.

"Are you two all right with taking care of the body?"

"Sure, Chan," Caleb said. "Is Ruby inside?"

"With the other woman Burris brutalized," Beth answered.

Mack knelt to take a closer look at Burris. "So this is the man who shot Gabe. He should've ridden out instead of staying around to go after you. I wonder what he was doing in the Palace."

Chan smirked. "Keeping watch for me."

Gyp couldn't believe what he'd learned. Agent Cartman. He knew from Simon she worked with Agent Thaddeus Taylor, two of the best counterfeit investigators the government had.

There was just one reason Cartman would be in Splendor. They'd somehow tracked the shipments to the small frontier town. He wondered if they'd discovered the printer, or the people who shipped the fake notes.

Passing the jail, he headed down the boardwalk toward the telegraph office. He needed to get a message to Simon. That was when Gyp remembered the telegram in his pocket.

Taking a seat on a nearby bench, he pulled it out, confirming he was alone. He deciphered the simple code and read it quickly, then once more. He'd been planning to ride off on his own with the package of notes in his saddlebag. Simon's telegram changed his mind.

The Priests were offering him an additional ten percent to run their operations in the west, which included Splendor and Denver. That would give him a fifteen percent share, triple what he made now.

He'd thought of asking for another five percent, but not ten. Even though it meant more work, he couldn't afford to walk away now.

If the operations continued to be successful, he'd be a rich man within five years. Enough to buy a house overlooking the San Francisco Bay and retire.

Gyp didn't have the desire to funnel some of his share to the Southern cause, an effort which hadn't ended in success the first time, leaving many loyal men dead.

Everything he made would go into his personal stash, not to be touched until he left the company of the

Priest brothers. Unlike what he'd planned even an hour ago, it would be an amicable parting.

Folding the paper, he slid it back into a pocket. This meant the issue of Agent Cartman was now his responsibility. Whatever Simon and Damien decided, Gyp would be in charge of carrying out their orders.

Leaning back, he considered the telegram to the Priests. The brothers had little patience and no love for anyone associated with what they considered the Union government.

Their strong beliefs had caused problems in the past. Gyp was certain what he had to tell them would trigger a quick, possibly explosive response. The telegram had to be worded right to lessen the impact. He needed them to be reasonable, which meant not ordering the death of Agent Cartman. An order Gyp had no desire to carry out.

Chan and Beth watched the man they knew as Tom Smith from their position across the street. As expected, he'd passed the jail in his hurry to get away from them. They'd found him seated on a bench, watched as he retrieved what appeared to be a telegram from a pocket and read. He hadn't hidden his surprise at the contents.

"Something about Mr. Smith doesn't seem right to me."

Beth nodded, continuing to watch the man across the street. "I agree. Most men who'd killed someone would be distraught. Not him. It was as if he'd done it enough that it didn't bother him."

Chan let out a breath, stroking his stubbled jaw. "My thoughts, too. And I'd wager his name isn't Tom Smith."

"He could've done a lot better with his alias. So who is he and why is he in Splendor?"

"It may be he came here to do exactly what happened."

Beth glanced at him, a brow raised. "Kill Burris?"

"Makes sense. He happened to be nearby when Burris jumped out the window."

"The outlaw dropped right down in front of him."

Chan nodded. "Smith drew a gun and killed him. Look."

Beth watched as Smith walked into the telegraph office. "Now he's sending a telegram to whoever hired him about completing the job."

"We could also be completely wrong and he came here for something else," Chan said.

"What we need is for Bernie to tell us who's the recipient of the telegram."

Chan snorted at the absurd notion. "Bernie has too much pride in his job to go outside the usual process."

"Then we have to find another way to learn Smith's true identity and why he's in Splendor."

Chan's gaze narrowed on the door of the telegraph office. "And discover the name of the person who hired him."

Chapter Twenty-Seven

"This is highly irregular, Marshal." Bernie's eyes flashed in defiance at the unorthodox request. Chan and Beth had requested the name of the person receiving Tom Smith's telegram. "Quite against the rules," he huffed, drumming his fingers on the counter.

"Mr. Smith shot and killed a man who roughed up Ruby Walsh and one of her girls. He then shot at us before jumping out a window. Agent Cartman and I believe Smith did it on the orders of someone else. We need the name, Bernie."

Letting out an exasperated breath, he picked up his log. "He sent two telegrams. One to Bob Jones in Omaha. The second went to Bill Jones in Kansas City." Closing the ledger, he glared between them. "Don't ask me what he wrote." His body bobbed up and down, gaze darting about the small space.

Chan ignored the comment. "Was there anything illegal in the message?"

"I just said—"

Chan interrupted him. "All I'm asking is if the message included anything that could be interpreted as against the law."

Bernie shook his head. "Not that I could tell. Fact is, both telegrams were the same except for the name of the recipients."

Glancing at Beth, he turned back to Bernie. "Thank you for your help."

"Sure, Marshal. Anything you want." Letting out a breath, his Adam's apple bobbed up and down as he watched the pair leave.

"*Anything you want, Marshal.*" Beth imitated Bernie, smiling at Chan.

"He's just doing his job."

"I know. Still, we are trying to figure out if someone is a killer."

"It's not enough for him to break the rules, Beth. He gave us more than I expected. We know Smith sent telegrams to Bob and Bill Jones in Omaha and Kansas City."

"Two cities Thad suspects of being central points in the counterfeiting ring."

Chan gave a slow nod. "Isn't Thad in Kansas City?"

They hadn't gotten fifty feet down the boardwalk when Bernie's voice had them turning around. "Marshal!"

"What is it?"

Lowering his voice, Bernie glanced around, hands rubbing up and down his thighs. "I was thinking about what you said about Smith maybe being an outlaw."

Chan placed his hands on his hips, growing impatient when Bernie hesitated. "And?"

"I remember him being in Splendor a few months ago, but he didn't call himself Tom Smith."

"What name did he use?"

"Well, I only have the last name. Slade. He sent a telegram to a man named Simon in Omaha. Could be this Bob Jones is the same man."

Beth sucked in a breath, the color draining from her face.

"What is it?" Chan asked.

Licking her lips, she took a step away. "It's nothing."

Narrowing his gaze, Chan studied her face. She was a terrible liar. "Thank you, Bernie. That's real good information."

"Anytime, Marshal." He hurried away, waving to people he knew before disappearing into the telegraph office.

Jaw clenched, Chan clasped Beth's elbow. "We need to talk."

"Don't we have other people to talk to? And don't you want to check the wanted posters in the jail for someone with a last name of Slade? Or first name of Simon?"

"That can wait until after we talk." He guided her to the St. James and up the stairs to her room, holding out his hand for a key.

"You aren't coming inside."

Not responding, he took the key when she drew it out of her reticule. Unlocking the door, he followed her inside.

Whirling toward him, she crossed her arms. "Chan, you can't be in here."

"It's a little late for that, isn't it, Beth?"

Face reddening, she bit her lower lip. He was right, which she refused to admit. "What do you want?"

"We're going to talk. I'm going to ask questions and you're going to answer them."

"About what?"

"About Simon and Damien Priest."

The bravado faded with the knowledge Chan knew something about the brothers. Still, she wasn't ready to surrender. "Who?"

Grabbing a chair, he sat down, stretching out his long legs. "You're a lousy liar, Beth. It would be best if you told me what you know of the Priest brothers. I won't leave until you do."

She almost laughed. Now that he was inside her room, Beth didn't want him to leave. Another fact she wouldn't admit.

"Sit down and tell me what you know."

Not ready to go against Thad's orders and tell him, she sat on the edge of the bed. "How do you know about them?"

"Sheriff Parker Sterling held Simon Priest in the Big Pine jail, awaiting trial for murdering the sheriff in Moosejaw. Some men broke him out the night before the trial. Sterling told me what he knew about the Priest brothers, which wasn't much. Who are they, Beth, and how do you know them?"

Letting out a defeated breath, she clasped her hands in her lap. "Thad has believed for a while they're somehow involved in the forgery trade. Their names have appeared several times in the investigations, but nothing specific enough to make arrests."

"Explain what you have."

Tucking strands of hair behind her ears, she met his gaze. "Thad believes they're the leaders of a group trying to revive the Southern cause by building a treasury."

"To wage another war?" Incredulity laced his words.

"Yes. Thad thinks they're raising funds through the passing of fake notes. Unfortunately, we don't have enough for a case."

"What does he have to suggest they're behind this?"

"It's all circumstantial."

Exasperated, he straightened, leaning forward to rest his arms on his thighs. "I want to know all you and Thad have learned."

Nodding, she stood, pacing to the window. "Thad is the one who discovered most of what we know, and it's been since he left us in Big Pine."

Anger rushed through Chan at being left out of important information. Forcing himself to shove it aside, he nodded for her to continue.

"Damien Priest has been shipping paper, ink, and other supplies to Denver. From there, half the supplies were sent on to Splendor. The shipments to Denver have been going on for at least two years. To Splendor, several months."

"Which would be about the time Bernie says Slade, Smith, or whatever his name is was in Splendor."

"Yes."

"Anything else?"

"Isn't that enough?"

Chan lifted a brow, waiting.

"All right. There was something else. Simon was spotted in Milwaukee by one of the other agents Thad sometimes works with. The agent was following other leads when he saw Priest and followed him. He made several visits to the post office, as well as met with some known criminals. People with a history of being coney dealers. When the agent approached them, they denied knowing Simon."

"So it would be their word against the agent's."

"Correct, but it gave us a lead to the Priest brothers. At the same time, others have come forward to admit they were raising funds for another attack on the Union. It's just a matter of time before we gather all we need to arrest Simon, Damien, and their associates."

"Only if we can connect them to the source in Splendor," Chan said. "All we have to do is follow Slade."

"To the people printing the fake notes."

Instead of answering, Chan stood, stalking toward her. Reaching the bed, he stared down at her.

"Is that everything, Beth?"

Looking up, her chin jutted out, defiance in her eyes. "Yes."

"Good." Instead of turning away, his hands gripped her arms.

Her eyes were wide as he gently pulled her up to face him. "What are you doing?"

Instead of answering, he settled his mouth over hers, both hands moving to her back. After several long moments, he drew away. A satisfied grin broke across his face at her glassy eyes and swollen lips.

Kissing her once more, Chan stepped away, his voice thick and ragged. "It's time we finished this, Beth."

Blinking, she brushed fingers over her lips. "Finish?"

"Follow Slade and bring the investigation to a close. Then you can go back to your life, and I'll go on with mine."

Her chest squeezed, heart breaking at his words. She'd foolishly thought they might have a chance for a future. Thought he still loved her. How wrong she'd been.

Pushing past him, she picked up her reticule and walked to the door. "You're right. I can't wait to get out of here and back to my *real* life."

Beth felt sick to her stomach and sick at heart. Neither one would she let Chan see. Head high, hand moving to touch the hidden pocket revolver in her dress, she headed outside, more than ready to locate Smith.

"We should split up."

Chan reached out, grabbing her arm to stop her. "Are you all right?"

"Of course." She scanned the street, looking everywhere except at Chan. "If we split up, we can cover more ground and locate Slade faster."

"No."

"What do you mean *no*?"

"I mean we are not going to split up. He killed a man today, Beth. There's no reason he won't kill you if he realizes he's being followed."

"I can take care of myself, Chan. You being with me doesn't guarantee my safety. Now, which part of town do you want to take?"

Removing his hat, he threaded a hand through his hair, frustration rolling through him. "Whatever part you want. I'm not leaving you alone." Slamming his hat back on his head, he glared down at her. "I don't know what's going on in that pretty head of yours, but you're stuck with me, Beth."

Turning, she walked away. "Not for long, Marshal Evans," she whispered to herself.

Chapter Twenty-Eight

Chan didn't understand what he'd done to anger Beth. He'd been doing all he could to let her know how much he wanted her, cared about her. Not once had she expressed anything more than desire. It was Austin all over again.

This time, he'd prepared himself for her to leave. Expected it to happen. He didn't understand why voicing the inevitable would upset her, but something had, and that was all it could be.

"Let's start on this street and move farther out. We should check the saloons, hotels, and restaurants."

Still angry about Chan insisting on going with her, she marched down the street, heading toward Noah's livery. They looked inside each of the shops, saloons, everywhere without a sign of Smith.

Neither spoke as they searched. After their conversation in the hotel room, all she wanted was to find the man, follow him, and discover where the printing press was hidden.

She knew the stage came through three times one week, four times the next. An odd schedule, but it worked for the residents of Splendor. Beth planned to be on it as soon as possible.

"Let's go to the next street." Chan did all he could to focus on the search, finding it hard with Beth so close. Back straight, hand poised at the opening to the pocket holding her pistol, he didn't want to think about losing her again.

Slowing when they reached the street where the clinic and Ruby's Palace were located, both stopped. "Which way first?" Beth asked.

"We'll go left, circle around, and end up at the clinic."

Following his instructions, she walked past the back doors of several businesses facing the main street, then past a row of houses used by Mack, Caleb, and the schoolteacher. The clinic was next.

On a whim, not believing the man would be inside, they opened the door. As suspected, the only people waiting around were Walter Evans, Noah Brandt, Nora, Mack, and Caleb. Chan was surprised to see the deputies.

"What's happening?" Chan knew Nick had taken Suzanne and their son home that morning.

"Doc Worthington says we can take Gabe home," his father said. "Lena is in his room with the baby. Mack and Caleb have offered to help."

Chan knew Noah had barely left the clinic since the shooting. "When can he leave?"

"Anytime now. Noah will bring around a wagon once the doctor comes out." The instant the words left Walter's mouth, Doc Worthington walked out. He looked at Noah.

"Go ahead and get the wagon. He'll be ready by the time you return." Sitting down, he scrubbed a hand over his face. "You understand he isn't going to be a docile patient." The comment made everyone laugh.

"How can I help?" Chan asked.

Nora lifted a brow, smiling. "You can hold the baby while we get Gabe and Lena settled."

The look of horror on Chan's face had everyone laughing again. Holding up his hands, he backed away.

"I'll help get them into the wagon while you hold the baby, Nora."

Beth spoke for the first time. "Have they selected a name?"

"Like Nick and Suzanne, they want to wait until they're home. Is it all right if I go into the room, Doctor?"

"I don't see why not, Walter. You can help dress him."

"Haven't done that since Gabe was five." He chuckled, heading into the room.

When Noah returned, Chan and the deputies carried a quarrelsome Gabe outside, loading him into the back of the wagon. Walter and Nora helped Lena onto the wagon seat, handing her the tiny bundle.

Chan jumped into the back of the wagon, his hand on Gabe's shoulder, ignoring his brother's protests about not being an invalid. Noah slapped the lines, drawing Chan's attention to those standing outside the clinic.

Beth was nowhere in sight. Straightening, he twisted around to scan the street ahead and behind them. He saw no sign of her.

Cursing under his breath, Chan shifted back down, leaning his back against the wagon. She hadn't been happy about looking for the man they now knew to be Slade, together. It was obvious Beth wanted little to do with him after he'd mentioned her leaving.

"Then you can go back to your life, and I'll go on with mine."

He winced at the reminder of his words. They hadn't come out as he'd meant. Cold and unfeeling, not at all what he felt about Beth. And she'd responded in kind.

"You're right. I can't wait to get out of here and back to my real life."

It now seemed she'd gone off on her own to find Slade. A dangerous situation when the man they hunted had killed a man that morning.

Tapping down his unease, Chan's jaw clenched at her being out there unprotected. He'd get Gabe and Lena settled inside their home, then borrow one of his brother's horses. The sooner he returned to town, the sooner he could protect the woman who had no use for his protection.

Beth moved carefully around town, tense but aware of those around her. She'd gotten a decent look at Slade, certain she'd be able to identify him.

Anger and disappointment hung heavily inside her. Anger at allowing herself to fall back in love with Chan

Evans, and disappointment the lawman didn't return her feelings.

Their attraction had always been explosive. After being married, becoming used to a man's strong arms holding her at night, being with Chan felt natural. It had surprised her how fast and hard she'd fallen for him. It had taken months to feel the same for Abner, which was why she'd left Chan in Austin. A mistake she regretted every single day.

Their reunion in Big Pine had been unexpected, yet she'd welcomed the chance to explain why leaving had been the only choice at the time. A part had also hoped Chan would forgive her, perhaps even giving them a second chance.

Instead, he'd been kind, a wonderful and sensitive lover while knowing another chance wasn't something he could provide. She'd offered herself freely, and now she'd be leaving him behind a second time. Not her choice.

Hearing boots pounding on the boardwalk behind her, she moved aside, relieved it was an older man with no resemblance to Slade. An odd reaction when she'd been trying to find him.

Slipping a hand into her pocket, she continued walking, being even more vigilant. Anxious to close the investigation and leave, she picked up her pace. She wondered how long it would be before Chan finished with his family and started looking for her. Not long, she guessed.

Up ahead, a tall, slender, man crossed the street, disappearing between two buildings. More wiry than muscled, his blond hair peeked from under his brown cowboy hat. She was certain it was Slade.

Trying not to draw attention, she quickened her pace, stopping at the corners of the buildings. She didn't see him. Unwilling to give up, she rushed down the small space. It ended on the street where several deputies and both doctors lived with their families.

A bittersweet smile twisted her lips. In a short time, Chan had educated her on many people in Splendor. Knowledge she tried to remember as she tracked Slade.

Seeing no reason he'd spend his time on a residential street, she ran to the next one. It opened to the back of buildings in the Chinatown area. Not seeing him, she hurried to the front of the buildings.

Standing a few stores away with his hands on his hips, Slade stared through the window of a Chinese bookstore. The one she and Chan had visited trying to find any trace they printed the forged notes. They'd found nothing, but hadn't crossed them off their list. Unless there was another printing press in Splendor, the notes had to be produced in the bookstore or the newspaper office.

Slowing her steps, she tried to look natural as she passed stores in an area of town few non-Asians visited. She and Abner had visited New York's growing Chinatown, buying spices and herbs. They'd been fascinated by the medicines they sold, Abner buying a few for headaches and stomach pain. The area in Splendor was much smaller, but still had many of the same stores.

Trying to watch him without drawing his attention, she stared through the window of the herb shop. From the corner of her eye, Beth saw him enter the bookshop. Moving to the corner of the store, she peeked inside.

Slade stood near the back counter, speaking to the owner. The same man who'd shown her and Chan their printing press.

She dashed back down the boardwalk when Slade turned to leave. Beth didn't know if he'd already spotted her, but couldn't take the chance. She had to continue following, not wanting to run the risk of losing him.

Beth dashed back to the herb shop, looking through the window again. Next door was a general store, selling many of the same types of items carried at Petermann's General Store. Dry goods, canned food, clothing, shoes, and boots, all with labels in Chinese.

Beth would like to come back another time when she wasn't following someone. That wouldn't happen. Within a few days, a week at most, she'd be on a stage, never returning to Splendor. The thought made a hard ball of regret form in her chest.

Shaking it off, she stiffened when Slade approached. Beth didn't pretend he wouldn't recognize her from their encounter outside of Ruby's Palace. He surprised her, though.

Slade walked right past her, showing no sign of recognition. Relaxing, Beth stayed where she was until he turned to head back toward the main street. She wondered if his next stop would be the office of the Splendor Herald.

Cautious, believing if he spotted her again he'd know she followed and would disappear, she decided to stay farther behind. Approaching the main street, she slowed, looking one way, then the other.

Slade stood outside Suzanne's boardinghouse, glancing around before going inside. It wasn't where she expected him to go. Beth had been certain he'd go straight to the newspaper office, unless all her instincts were wrong. Then again, Chan believed if the fake bills originated in Splendor, they were printed in Chinatown, not by the owners of the Splendor Herald.

Frustrated, she passed the general store, barber shop, gunsmith, and jail, keeping her attention on the boardinghouse across the street. Maybe he was staying there, or going inside for a meal. Regardless, she had to find a place to wait and watch. Someplace he wouldn't notice her and Chan wouldn't see her.

Beth didn't know why it was so important to do this alone. She'd never been one to seek praise for a successful job. In fact, she'd never sought any type of acclaim, preferring to focus on the next assignment.

Abner was the same, more intent on the next lead and arresting criminals than accolades from his superiors. Thad wanted both. Locking up lawbreakers and gaining the admiration of those in the government meant a great deal to him. His wealth meant little to Thad. His motivation came from being recognized for his own achievements, not those of his wealthy ancestors.

Before she could find a suitable place to observe Slade, Chan's hard-edged voice came from a few feet away.

"Where have you been? And don't lie to me, Beth. I'll know if you do."

Chapter Twenty-Nine

Beth took a step away, glaring at Chan and his overbearing behavior. She didn't report to him and owed him nothing more than what he'd be willing to share with her.

Placing fisted hands on her hips, she felt her face heat. "What makes you believe I'd lie to you?"

Crossing his arms, he glared back at her. "Maybe because you didn't share what you knew about the Priest brothers." He didn't feel any satisfaction when she flinched. "Have you found Slade?"

She thought about not answering, tossing aside the ridiculous notion. "He's in the boardinghouse."

Chan shifted to look down the street. "Is he staying there?"

She shrugged, shaking her head. "I followed him to Chinatown. He went inside the bookstore, stayed a few minutes, then left. You may be right and the operation is coming out of the Chinese store."

Chan nodded, running a hand over his face. "He didn't see you?"

"He may have, but didn't recognize me."

Chan continued to watch the boardinghouse. "You should've waited for me."

"You had an obligation to your family. One of us had to continue looking for Slade."

He hated she was right. They couldn't give up the search because of duty to his family. Beth had done what he would've—continued looking for Smith, determining if he was involved in the counterfeiting.

"Did he go into the newspaper office?"

"No. I thought he would, but…" Her shoulders slumped from exhaustion.

"It doesn't matter, Beth. We'll continue to keep watch on Slade and be patient. He may still lead us right to the coney man." A quick glance over his shoulder had him grabbing her arm. "Come on."

"What?" She looked at the boardinghouse. Slade emerged, settling his hat on his head as he walked toward them from the other side of the street.

He all but dragged her into the jail, closing the door before moving to the window. They watched as the man walked into the Dixie.

"What's going on?" Beau joined them at the window, chewing on a piece of jerky.

"There's a man in town we believe is involved with the counterfeiting operation," Chan answered, his gaze never wavering from the saloon.

"What can I do to help?"

"Go to the Dixie and keep watch on him," Chan answered. "He told us his name is Tom Smith, but we believe him to be an outlaw named Gyp Slade. Tall and wiry with blond hair. He's the one who shot Burris."

Stuffing the jerky into a pocket, Beau pulled out his six-shooter, checking the cylinder. "How dangerous is he?"

"According to Slade, Burris drew on him. He was protecting himself. I checked wanted posters and found nothing under Tom Smith."

"Probably not his real name." Beau walked to the door.

"There *was* a poster for a Gyp Slade," Chan said. "I'm certain that's his real name."

Beau gave a quick nod. "Got to be the same man. I'll let you know if I learn anything."

They didn't relax until the deputy strode inside the Dixie.

"Are we watching the right person?" Beth clasped her hands in front of her, brows furrowed as she continued to stare across the street. When Chan didn't answer, she glanced up, surprised to see his intense gaze on her.

"I'm definitely watching the right person." Leaning down, he brushed a kiss across her lips. He would've taken it a little further except the door opened, Caleb and Cash walking inside. It took a couple minutes to explain about Slade, and Beau going to the Dixie.

"Have you told Enoch?" Cash asked.

Chan's mouth twisted in a grimace. "I hadn't thought about it."

"I'll find him. He's the perfect one to follow. No one expects the town drunk of watching and remembering," Cash said.

Chan's brow lifted. "But he's been sober."

Caleb chuckled, stepping to the window to look at the Dixie. "Very few people know that. It's an excellent cover."

Beth moved aside to let Cash look outside. "I've never seen one of the Chinese go into the Dixie or Wild Rose."

"Chinese?" Chan opened the jail door.

"Lee Yang, the man who owns several shops in Chinatown," answered Cash.

"Which ones?"

Cash rubbed his chin. "I'm pretty sure the general store, herb shop, and bookstore."

Beth touched Chan's arm. "We've got the connection."

"Let's get back to the bookstore before he returns. Are you two all right keeping watch here?"

Caleb nodded.

"I'll still find Enoch." Cash headed outside, then stopped. "He may have seen something that will help."

Chan believed they'd already found the link. Smith had visited the bookstore earlier. Now the owner had sought him out at the saloon. He hoped Beau would be able to overhear their conversation.

"Let's go, Beth." Taking her hand, they left Caleb in the jail.

Hurrying to Chinatown, they ducked into the shop, heading straight to the back. Two men stood around the printer.

Shouting and pointing at them, the two backed away, one reaching for a metal lance against one wall. Brandishing it at Chan, he balanced himself on the balls of his feet, continuing to yell at them in Chinese.

By the way he glared at them while wielding the spear, it was clear they weren't welcome. Drawing his gun, Chan shot a bullet into the floor. The one holding the lance jumped away, as did the other.

"Where is the second press?" Chan returned the gun to its holster.

The men looked at each other, shaking their heads. A second shot caused the one to drop his makeshift weapon, the other to cower in a corner.

Looking around, Chan and Beth sought anything indicating a hatch to a basement or door to an attic. They found neither.

Unwilling to give up, they searched the shelves and cupboards once more. "There has to be something," Beth said. "Why else would Lee Yang go to the Dixie?"

"No reason at all. You heard Cash," Chan said. "It's rare the Chinese go into the Dixie or Wild Rose. It's too much of a coincidence Smith would visit this shop and Lee Yang would go directly to the saloon within an hour. He had to tell someone here he'd be there and to pass it on to Yang."

"And he immediately went to find him," Beth said.

"There's no reason for them to meet unless they're partners in the forgery ring."

She nodded, not stopping her search. "There's nothing here. If they do print fake notes, they're good at hiding the plates, special inks, and paper."

They straightened at the sound of the front door opening and closing. The two men in back resumed their shouting. Lee Yang burst into the back a moment later, face red, eyes blazing in anger.

"What you want?"

Chan glanced at Beth, then back at Lee Yang. "Why did you meet with Tom Smith?"

If Yang was surprised, he didn't show it. Instead, he approached Chan, pointing to the front of the store. "Out!"

Chan didn't budge. "Can't do that until we get answers."

"No answers. You leave. Now." Again, he pointed, but Chan didn't move.

"Who is Tom Smith?"

Yang shook his head. "No Tom Smith."

Brows furrowing, Chan took a step closer. "What do you mean no Tom Smith?"

"Don't know Tom Smith."

Beth crossed her arms, jaw set. "We saw you go into the Dixie to meet Smith."

Yang shook his head, staring at them as if they were deranged. "A man come here. Ask for me. Name not Smith."

"What is his name?" Chan asked.

"He said no tell."

"I'm a U.S. Marshal, Mr. Yang. Agent Cartman works for the federal government. We *do* have the authority to take you to jail until you decide to give us the name."

He must've understood as he crossed his arms, mouth drawing into a firm line. "If I tell, he kill me."

"Then it's jail." Chan pulled handcuffs from a back pocket.

"No. You wait," Yang said.

"Not unless you tell us his name."

Yang glared at Chan, his lips pursed tight.

"Your choice." He grabbed Yang by a shoulder, turning him around. "Put your hands behind you."

Yang stood frozen, as if not understanding. When he didn't move, Chan gripped one arm, then the other, securing them behind his back.

"Let's go."

"No, no. I do nothing wrong."

"If that's true, tell us the man's name and why he wanted to talk to you."

Hanging his head, Yang muttered something in Chinese. One of his men ran to the front, changed the sign to *Closed,* and locked the door.

"All right. It's time to talk."

"I no criminal."

"Understood, Yang." Chan glanced at Beth, both knowing that was still to be determined.

"He want me to print." Yang looked at them. "Not legal printing."

"How do you know it wasn't legal?" Chan asked.

Glancing away, he looked at his men before answering. "Bad money."

Working to hide his excitement, Chan sucked in a slow breath. "What do you mean by *bad money*?"

"You call fake notes. I tell him no and not come back. I honest man."

"Good decision, Mr. Yang," Beth said.

Chan's heart pounded, knowing they were so close. "Now, tell me his name."

Chapter Thirty

"Gyp Slade."

Chan and Beth stared at Yang. Now they had the confirmation they needed on the man's name. And his connection to the counterfeiting ring.

Releasing the handcuffs, Chan shoved them into a pocket. "Thank you, Mr. Yang. You've been very helpful."

Nodding at Beth, they headed to the front, Yang following. Unlocking the door, he let them pass before yelling after them. "I good man. Honest man."

They heard, but didn't respond as they raced toward the main street. Ducking into the jail, they joined Caleb at the window.

"Anything?" Chan asked.

"Beau hasn't returned, and Smith hasn't left the Dixie."

"Slade," Beth said. "Yang confirmed the man's name is Gyp Slade."

"He also told us Slade tried to talk him into printing forged notes," Chan said. "Yang turned him down."

Beth glanced back out the window. "We did check, and he doesn't have the supplies he'd need to print fakes."

"What does that do to your investigation?" Caleb asked.

Chan's jaw clenched. "There's another press in town. One we've missed."

"What about Lewis Gibson? He prints the Herald."

Beth shook her head. "We searched his place already, Caleb, and didn't find anything."

"So you believe there's a third press in town. I haven't seen another delivered, but Suzanne or Gabe would be the ones to ask."

Before Chan could reply, he spotted Gyp Slade leave the Dixie. He looked around, then walked to the other end of town, going inside the boardinghouse.

"What is Slade up to?" Beth whispered more to herself than anyone else.

The door opening drew their attention. Cash walked in, placing his hat on a hook and sitting down.

"Enoch is going to watch Smith."

"We found out his name is Gyp Slade, Cash," Chan said.

Going around the desk, the deputy pulled wanted posters from a drawer, rifling through them. After a moment, he held one up.

"Gyp Slade. Wanted for robbing stagecoaches and banks." He handed it to Chan. "Is this your man?"

"It's him, all right." Chan didn't admit he'd already seen the poster.

"Based on this, we can arrest him. Not wait until you connect him to the counterfeiters," Caleb said.

"No." Beth's response had them looking at her. "We need to use him to confirm a connection to the Priest brothers."

She explained Thad's theory and Bernie's recollection of mail from several months before. "If we arrest Slade for current charges, we may never be able to identify them as the leaders of the forgery ring."

Massaging the back of his neck, Caleb lowered himself into a chair. "All right. What do we do next?"

"Follow him without being noticed. We need to find out if he's made contact with Lewis Gibson or leads us to another press no one knows about." Beth twisted to look out the window. "Notes are being forged in Splendor. It's up to us to find the source."

Chan and Beth sat at a table at Suzanne's, both picking at their suppers. Between Gabe's deputies, Enoch, and the possibility Slade would recognize them, they had little to do but stand aside and wait.

"Do you think it's Lewis and his son?"

Chan looked up from his plate. "I don't know. My instincts tell me forgeries are being printed in Splendor and Gyp Slade is part of it. Unless there's another press, Lewis has to be involved."

"Not the Chinese?"

He shook his head. "Doesn't make sense."

Beth scooped up some mashed potatoes, lifting it to her mouth when Chan's next words stopped her.

"I love you, Beth, and I don't want you to leave."

Lowering the fork, the heaviness in her chest had her sucking in a slow breath. It took a moment before she could meet his expectant gaze. What she saw had her heart squeezing.

"If you go, I'll follow. I'm not letting you leave so easily this time."

Placing both hands in her lap, she clasped them together. "I'm a federal agent, Chan."

"And an excellent one."

"What would happen if I did stay?"

Staring at her, he braced his arms on the table, leaning toward her. "What do you want to happen?" Chan watched her eyes dart away from him, his hope of Beth deciding to stay beginning to fade. Swallowing the lump of dread in his throat, he tried again. "Do you love me?"

Returning her attention to him, she slowly met his gaze. "Yes."

He latched onto her confession, his voice rough. "Then stay. Build your future here...with me."

She wanted to say yes, tell him she never wanted to leave him again.

"Unless you don't love me enough to change your life. I know it's a lot to ask. I'm gone a good deal of time. When I'm not traveling between here, Big Pine, and the prison near Deer Lodge, I work on a ranch. It's nothing like your life in New York and Washington."

He didn't tell her he planned to buy his own land, build a house, and raise cattle. Nor did she know about his sizable inheritance. When the time was right, he'd quit his job as a marshal and use some of the money to build his own dreams. But it wouldn't be back east. Chan would build his home in Splendor.

Sweeping strands of hair from her face, Beth watched various emotions cross his face. "I like my job." Her voice held none of the conviction she expected.

"You could find a job here," Chan countered.

"Doing what?"

"Gabe is always looking for new deputies."

"I know nothing about being a deputy. Besides, I have nowhere to live."

Chan jerked. "You'd stay with me, Beth."

Her face flushed with indignation. "Having you sleep in my bed at the hotel is very different than moving in with you. I'd never be accepted if I flaunted propriety by openly living with you."

"Not if we're married."

Eyes wide, her mouth dropped open before closing. "You want to marry me?"

Reaching toward her, he placed his hand over hers. "Did I forget that part?"

She let out a broken laugh, moisture forming in her eyes. "I believe you did, Marshal Evans." Beth drew in a sharp breath when Chan shoved back his chair, dropping to his knees. Ignoring the startled stares of the other diners, he took both her hands.

"I love you Elizabeth Cartman. I want to share my life with you. Would you do me the honor of becoming my wife?"

"I—"

A loud explosion shook the windows, screams from those around them stopping whatever else Beth meant to say.

Standing, he drew his gun. "Stay here, Beth."

"I'm going with you." She pulled the pistol from her pocket, holding it at her side.

"Beth…"

"We're wasting time." Rushing past him, she shoved the door open, Chan right behind her. They focused on the smoke coming from just beyond the Dixie.

"It's the newspaper," Chan said, running toward it.

Dodging people hovering along the sides of the buildings, they arrived the same time as Hex, Zeke, and Dutch. People had already lined up to throw water on the blaze and the surrounding buildings.

"Are Lewis and his son still inside?" Nick joined them, tossing a bucket of water on the fire.

"We don't know yet." Hex tried to get closer to the building, holding up his arms and stepping back from the intense heat.

"Stop!"

Chan's shout caused everyone to turn. Gyp Slade headed south, past the church and new community building, kicking his horse to go faster.

Firing into the air, he yelled again. Shoving the weapon into the holster, he ran to the nearest horse, swinging into the saddle. Focused on catching up to Slade, Chan didn't notice Beth doing the same until they were outside the town limit.

Hearing the pounding of hooves behind him, Chan glanced over his shoulder, cursing. She was a few yards back, not losing ground as they followed Slade. All he could do now was do his best to keep Beth safe.

Following the trail, Chan spotted Slade at least a hundred yards ahead. The outlaw had slowed down, believing he'd lost anyone who followed. Or thinking no one tracked him.

Reining the horse into the cover of thick bushes and trees, Chan waved so Beth would know to stay with him. Using simple hand signals, he indicated what he planned to do and how she could help.

His intention was to take Slade alive and question him about the counterfeiting operation run by the Priest brothers. More than anything, he wanted to keep Beth safe, which meant not letting her too close to Slade.

Chan indicated for her to follow when bullets whizzed between them. Dropping to the ground, they grabbed rifles from the scabbards before slapping the flanks of their horses.

More bullets came at them from another angle, causing the pair to rush behind the dense foliage. Raising their rifles, they scanned the area, looking for any sign of Slade.

Movement to his right had Chan shifting the weapon, aiming on a flash of sunlight on metal. Firing, he heard a groan and squeezed the trigger again. This time, a scream tore through the air.

"We need to get to him," Beth said, moving before Chan could stop her.

Swearing under his breath, he rushed after her. A deep moan led them behind a thick oak. Lying on the ground, Slade held his thigh, trying to stop the bleeding. A second wound to his shoulder went untreated.

Reaching under her skirt, Beth tore a long strip from her chemise. Using half to bind the wound on Slade's thigh, the other half to slow the bleeding from his shoulder, she looked at Chan.

"We need to get him to the clinic."

Turning, he whistled for Caesar, forgetting his horse was still at Noah's livery. "I'll be right back."

"Who the hell are you and why did you shoot me?"

Beth stared at him, stifling a groan of exasperation. "Because you shot at us, Slade."

"How do you know my name?"

Sneering, she tightened one of the bandages, getting a yelp of pain. "The wanted poster."

Chan rode up, the reins of her horse in one hand. "I don't know where his horse is. We'll put him on yours and you'll ride with me."

"I'm not going anywhere," Slade ground out.

"You're going to the clinic, then the jail. Afterward, you're going to answer every question we have about the counterfeiting operation and the Priest brothers," Chan said.

Fighting the pain, Slade's mouth twisted into a grimace. "I don't know what you're talking about."

"I almost forgot. If they were in the shop you blew up, you'll also be charged with the murders of Lewis and Franklin Gibson," Chan added.

A whinny had them watching as Slade's horse came toward them. Walking over, Chan went through the saddlebags, grasping a cylinder several inches long with a fuse at one end. He held it in front of him for Slade to see.

"That's not mine," the outlaw screamed.

"It's in *your* saddlebag."

"Someone put it there."

Beth tugged on the bandage around his thigh once more. "And that someone was *you*."

Epilogue

Two weeks later...

A large group of women crowded around Lena and Suzanne, taking turns holding the two babies. Nora put forth the idea of a naming celebration with family and close friends at Gabe and Lena's home. She and a few other women had brought it all together within two short weeks.

On the other side of the room, a group of men puffed on cigars and sipped whiskey, discussing the counterfeiting ring and Gyp Slade's conviction.

"You did a great job bringing in that criminal, Chan." Walter clasped his youngest son's shoulder, who beamed at the accomplishment.

"It wasn't just me, Father. Gyp wouldn't be in jail without Agent Cartman and Gabe's deputies."

"Well then, you should all get a commendation," Walter said.

Caleb, Mack, and Cash grinned at the idea. "I'd rather have time to take Allie on a trip to San Francisco," Cash responded, mentioning his wife, the owner of the local millinery shop.

Caleb laughed. "Good luck getting her away from her business."

"What about you, Chan?" Gabe asked. He still had to take it easy, but he was back working at the jail.

"I'm fine right here." Chan let his gaze wander to the women, one in particular.

Beth held the baby girl as if she were the most precious bundle in the world. To the Evans family, she was. Close to a month old, Gabe and Walter doted on her. Watching Beth whisper to the baby did something to Chan's insides, a longing he'd never experienced.

The last weeks had rushed by without further discussion of Chan's proposal. A situation he planned to rectify today.

Gabe followed his gaze, staying quiet about Beth. "You got Gyp to confess to the stagecoach and bank robberies, as well as tell us what he knows about Simon and Damien Priest." He shook his head. "I still find it hard to believe the mastermind behind the entire counterfeiting ring is the same colonel I heard about during the war."

"According to Gyp, he's obsessed with resurrecting the Confederacy and gaining independence," Cash said.

Mack shook his head. "It will never happen."

"I agree." Hex's attention focused on Chrissy McKenna standing by her young sister, Cici. Without their help the last few months, he'd never have been able to make it as a single father with a precocious daughter of five.

"Same here." Beau had also fought for the Confederacy, alongside Cash. "The South is still getting back together. It will be a long time before they fully recover."

The clinking of silverware on glass had the men turning toward the women. Nora stood next to Lena and Suzanne, each now holding their babies.

"Gabe and Nick, would you join us?"

Amusement passed between the two good friends as they walked to stand next to their wives. Each took their babies from the ladies' arms, gently rocking them.

"Thank all of you for coming to celebrate the naming of the newest residents of Splendor." Nora glanced at her husband, Wyatt. They'd been trying to start a family and hoped to have their own announcement soon. "Nick and Suzanne, would you mind going first?"

Stepping forward, Nick put his free arm around his wife, a goofy smile on his face. "Sweetheart, I'll let you do the honors."

Stroking the soft hair on their son's head, she looked at the group of family and friends. "We're naming him Newton, but we plan to call him Newt."

Applause and cheering followed, causing Suzanne to swipe an errant tear rolling down her cheek. Placing a kiss on her temple, Nick guided her a few feet away.

Nora finished applauding, then faced her brother. "Gabe and Lena, you're next."

Gabe did the same as Nick, putting an arm around his wife as they stepped forward. Leaning up, she whispered next to his ear. "You tell them our choice, Gabe."

He looked around, frowning. "Where's Jack?"

"I'm here, Father."

"We want you by us."

Jack's face brightened as he walked forward, standing between his parents.

Clearing his throat, Gabe let out a shaky breath. "As you might imagine, it took us a while to *agree* on a name." He waited a moment as the chuckles faded. "We finally came to an understanding last night. We've decided to name her Emmaline. Emma for short."

Shouts and more applause rang out, their friends converging around both couples. Chan stayed back. He'd have plenty of time to be with his niece. There was just one female he wanted to be near right now, and he couldn't see her.

"I think she went out front, son." Walter stood next to him, gently nudging Chan toward the front door.

Giving his father a brief nod, he tried not to run on his way to find her. Opening the door, he saw her standing by the front porch rail.

"Beth?"

She didn't turn around, resting her hands on the top of the rail. Chan stepped behind her, wrapping his arms around her waist. Sucking in a breath, she leaned against his hard chest, sighing.

Bending down, he placed kisses along her neck, feeling her shiver. "I love you, Beth."

"I know." Her voice was so low he almost missed it. Chan waited, holding his breath, hoping she'd say more. "I love you, too."

Relief overwhelmed him. Unable to control himself, he turned her toward him, cupping her face. "Marry me, Beth."

Moisture filled her eyes, threatening to spill over. Blinking, she caught her lower lip between her teeth, giving a slow nod.

A small smile tilted the corners of his mouth. "Is that a *yes*?"

Her smile was broad, brightening her entire face. "Yes, Chan. I'll marry you."

Picking her up, he swung her around on a loud whoop. A moment later, his family and some of the friends rushed outside, then stopped at the sight of the beaming couple.

"What's going on?" Gabe asked, still holding Emma.

Setting Beth down, Chan placed a possessive arm over her shoulders. "Everyone, Elizabeth Cartman has agreed to marry me!"

Thank you for taking the time to read Storm Summit. If you enjoyed it, please consider telling your friends or posting a short review. Word of mouth is an author's best friend and much appreciated.

Watch for book fifteen in the Redemption Mountain series, Mystery Mesa.

If you want in on all the backstage action of my historical westerns, join my VIP Reader's Group: https://geni.us/PzgXR

Join my Newsletter to be notified of Pre-Orders and New Releases: https://www.shirleendavies.com/

I care about quality, so if you find something in error, please contact me via email at shirleen@shirleendavies.com

About the Author

Shirleen Davies writes romance. She is the best-selling author of books in the romantic suspense, military romance, historical western romance, and contemporary western romance genres. Shirleen grew up in Southern California, attended Oregon State University, and has degrees from San Diego State University and the University of Maryland. Her passion is writing emotionally charged stories of flawed people who find redemption through love and acceptance. She lives with her husband in a beautiful town in northern Arizona.

I love to hear from my readers!

Send me an email: shirleen@shirleendavies.com
Visit my Website: www.shirleendavies.com
Sign up to be notified of New Releases:
www.shirleendavies.com
Check out all of my Books:
www.shirleendavies.com/books.html
Comment on my Blog:
www.shirleendavies.com/blog.html
Follow me on Amazon:
http://www.amazon.com/author/shirleendavies
Follow my on BookBub:
https://www.bookbub.com/authors/shirleen-davies

Other ways to connect with me:

Facebook Author Page:
http://www.facebook.com/shirleendaviesauthor
Twitter: www.twitter.com/shirleendavies
Pinterest: http://pinterest.com/shirleendavies
Instagram:
https://www.instagram.com/shirleendavies_author/

Books by Shirleen Davies
Historical Western Romance Series
MacLarens of Fire Mountain

Tougher than the Rest, Book One
Faster than the Rest, Book Two
Harder than the Rest, Book Three
Stronger than the Rest, Book Four
Deadlier than the Rest, Book Five
Wilder than the Rest, Book Six

Redemption Mountain

Redemption's Edge, Book One
Wildfire Creek, Book Two
Sunrise Ridge, Book Three
Dixie Moon, Book Four
Survivor Pass, Book Five
Promise Trail, Book Six
Deep River, Book Seven
Courage Canyon, Book Eight
Forsaken Falls, Book Nine
Solitude Gorge, Book Ten
Rogue Rapids, Book Eleven
Angel Peak, Book Twelve
Restless Wind, Book Thirteen
Storm Summit, Book Fourteen
Mystery Mesa, Book Fifteen, Coming next in the series!

MacLarens of Boundary Mountain

Colin's Quest, Book One,
Brodie's Gamble, Book Two
Quinn's Honor, Book Three
Sam's Legacy, Book Four
Heather's Choice, Book Five
Nate's Destiny, Book Six
Blaine's Wager, Book Seven
Fletcher's Pride, Book Eight
Bay's Desire, Book Nine
Cam's Hope, Book Ten

Romantic Suspense

Eternal Brethren, Military Romantic Suspense

Steadfast, Book One
Shattered, Book Two
Haunted, Book Three
Untamed, Book Four
Devoted, Book Five
Faithful, Book Six, Coming Next in the Series!

Peregrine Bay, Romantic Suspense

Reclaiming Love, Book One
Our Kind of Love, Book Two
Edge of Love, Coming Next in the Series!

<u>***Contemporary Romance Series***</u>

MacLarens of Fire Mountain

Second Summer, Book One
Hard Landing, Book Two
One More Day, Book Three
All Your Nights, Book Four
Always Love You, Book Five
Hearts Don't Lie, Book Six
No Getting Over You, Book Seven
'Til the Sun Comes Up, Book Eight
Foolish Heart, Book Nine

Burnt River

Thorn's Journey
Del's Choice
Boone's Surrender

The best way to stay in touch is to subscribe to my newsletter. Go to www.shirleendavies.com and subscribe in the box at the top of the right column that asks for your email. You'll be notified of new books before they are released, have chances to win great prizes, and receive other subscriber-only specials.

9 781947 680166